BIRDLAND

an entertainment in which might be found:
three Lucys... two of whom have a dog named Georgie,
two mynas, two magpies, and one, two or five kagus

Luciwa Peregrine

nuna

Pataphor: 1. An extended metaphor that creates its own context.
            2. That which occurs when a lizard's tail grows so long it drops off and grows a new lizard.

First published in New Zealand by Nuna 2021.

Copyright © Nuna on behalf of the author.
The moral right of the author has been asserted.

All rights reserved.
No part of this publication may be reproduced, stored in a retrieval system, or transmitted, in any form or by any means, without the prior permission in writing of the publisher, nor be circulated in any form of binding or cover other than that in which it is published and without a similar condition, including this condition, being imposed by the subsequent purchaser.

ISBN 9780473582852 (hardback)
ISBN 9780473582845 (paperback)
ISBN 9780473582876 (PDF)
ISBN 9780473582869 (EPUB)

Illustrations by the author
Typeset in Jansen Text by:
Nuna Gallery Press, Auckland, New Zealand
Printed and bound by IngramSpark
A catalogue record for this book is available from the National Library of New Zealand.

nuna
www.nunagallery.com

Pick a flower on Earth and you move the farthest star
—Paul Dirac

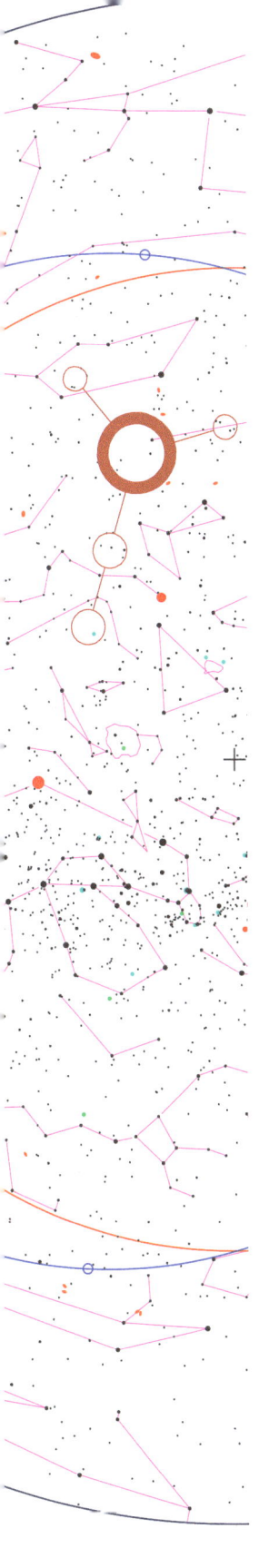

contents

book one || Birdland

one | Humpty
two | George Ballchaser III
three | Birdland
four | Bananas
five | Best in Show
six | Passerine Peninsula
seven | Airborne

book two || Falde

one | Arrival
two | Plumage
three | Academy
four | Flight
five | Shelter
six | Asylum
seven | Escape
eight | War
nine | Bird Sanctuary
ten | Flotsam

book three || Aves

one | Ruffled Feathers
two | Birds of a Feather
three | Midnight in Birdland
four | Quest
five | Nuna
six | Plumage II
seven | Bird in the Hand
eight | Breeding Programme

Epilogue | Flotsam

book one
Birdland

1 | Humpty

Humpty Dumpty sat on a wall,
Humpty Dumpty had a great fall.
In the history of falls, this fall was appalling,
for Humpty kept falling and falling and falling.

"Are you asleep… or pretending to be asleep, George Ballchaser the Third?" She peered over the top of the book.

George Ballchaser III was lying at the bottom of her bed. He was on his back with his legs flung out haphazardly. His eyes were firmly shut and an elastic smile stretched around his long hairy snout. She raised the book and continued reading aloud.

"I had no idea," he exclaimed on his tumble,
"This wall was so tall—it makes me feel humble.
To create such a wall takes a giant brick surplus…
Just how did it get here? And what is its purpose?"

Days soon ticked by as Humpty descended,
his thoughts grew profound just as nature intended.
He solved first the riddle of Humpty eggs-istence,
intuited gravity without assistance.

He came up with many exotic equations.
He worked out a system for hyper-inflations.
He wrote a great novel then made orchestrations.
He solved all the problems of egg-egg relations.

From years of this falling his mind was enlightened.
In darkness and space-time, he brightened and brightened.
By map or by app you can see him by night,
he's that bright twinkling star in the east, to the right...

She put her book down and nudged him with her foot.

"I know it's a bedtime story," she pretended to scowl, "but you could at least have waited until the end before you started snoring!" She leaned down and kissed him on the head, then fluffed up her pillow and turned off the light.

2 | George Ballchaser III

Lucy woke up with a wet nose. George Ballchaser III was licking it with his big pink tongue.

"Yucky!!!" she said, giggling. "You have some very bad habits, George Ballchaser the Third."

George Ballchaser III didn't seem to mind the insult. He wagged his tail and tried to plant another lick on her nose. This was how she woke up every morning, to equal measures of dog breath and dog slobber launched from very close range. Sleeping in was not something that George Ballchaser III approved of at all. It's fair to say that there was no chance of getting up late when George Ballchaser III was interested in an early start, which was every day.

Following a delicious breakfast of porridge with yoghurt and stewed tamarillos, which always tasted better in pyjamas, Lucy put on her yellow dress and selected a ball from the top drawer of her ball cabinet. It was the drawer marked *Very Bouncy*.

The other drawers in descending order were *Quite Bouncy*, *Some Occasional Bounce* and *Not Very Bouncy At All!* She chose the white ball with red polkadots which George Ballchaser III seemed to be especially fond of, then grabbed her sunhat, just in case, and ambled down the path from the front door to the driftwood gate where Mr Ballchaser III was waiting very patiently.

"Should we play in the clearing or go to the beach?" she asked him, opening the gate. Then she sighed dramatically with her hands on her hips, adding "Why do I waste my breath asking you anything at all, George Ballchaser the Third?"

As usual, George Ballchaser III was heading off toward the beach before she was even half way through her question. "A simple 'let's go to the beach again, Lucy' with a 'please' and a 'thank you very much' thrown in for the sake of good manners would be nice," she called to his wagging hind quarters as she closed the gate and skipped down the trail after him.

It should be mentioned that George Ballchaser III didn't speak much, in fact he never said anything that you might optimistically call a sentence, but he knew what he liked and even though the list of what he liked was quite long by ordinary dog standards, chasing balls on the beach was right at the top of that list.

It was a broad, white sandy beach that stretched away flat and straight in both directions. Above the high tide mark where the sand was loose and irregular, a scattering of logs, sticks, shells, dried seaweed and an assortment of other bits and pieces, even some coconuts, were remnants of a recent storm. The sea was shimmering with morning light, infused with a reddish glow. Out to the horizon it was calm and serene, but the tide still managed to conjure foamy heads on the little wavelets that surged up the sand.

Lucy made her way across the beach and stood between the tide marks where the sand was just firm enough for a ball to bounce. She jumped up and down a couple of times to check, then decided it was perfect. She tossed the polkadot ball as far as she could—which wasn't all that far she had to admit to herself—although it being a bouncy ball helped a lot. George Ballchaser III bounded after it as if his very life depended on setting a new land speed record. He picked it up in his mouth and raced back, dropping the ball at her feet with an expectant look.

Minor variations on this pattern constituted the fetch game. Lucy always had the impression that George Ballchaser III would happily play all day if he could find anyone as enthusiastic about throwing the ball as he was about chasing it.

As the game wore on, Lucy explained to him that the day after tomorrow would be her ninth birthday, making her five years older than him instead of just four. She thought George Ballchaser III looked quite impressed with that piece of news.

"Being nine will mean that I'll be more grown-up, of course," she said, placing a finger on her lips thoughtfully. "You know, it might not be appropriate for you to lick my nose every morning when I'm nine! I might let you do it sometimes but at the very least you should probably ask permission first."

George Ballchaser III looked up at her, then down at the ball near her feet, then up at her again, then back to the ball. He seemed not to be paying any real attention to what she was saying, or at least he was paying a lot of attention to the ball.

"It's all right if you don't want to talk about this right now, young dog, seeing as how it's your playtime…" she said in her most adult voice, "but don't think we've finished discussing this *Very Important Issue* yet. You have to have lots more rules when you're grown-up. That's what being grown-up means."

She picked up the ball and tossed it into the waves. George Ballchaser III looked at it bobbing on the water for a few moments then gave a little bark and bounded after it into the surf.

He had a jaunty paddling style, not something you'd see at the Olympic Games, but still quite efficient. The ball, though, seemed to be moving away from him just as fast as he was moving towards it, and both ball and dog were moving quickly away from where she was standing on the beach. As he got smaller and smaller, Lucy called to him to come back but he didn't seem to hear her. She was starting to get a little bit worried. What if he lost sight of the ball and just kept swimming in that direction, or if the ball never stopped moving away? What if he got it and turned around to come back and couldn't see the shore? Her little bit worried was quickly turning into a big bit worried. She looked up and down the beach.

Not far away was a small sailboat, mostly in the water with just its flat stern sitting on the sand. She ran over to it. It had white painted wooden sides and its name *Luciana* was in red paint on the bow. A main sail was attached to the mast and a small jib sail was strung from the mast to the prow. Lucy decided that it was just the right size for an 8-turning-9-year-old girl and her dog—once he'd been rescued, of course. She pushed at the stern and the boat slid easily off the sand so that it was floating free on the water, then she climbed aboard.

She had never sailed a boat before and she wasn't sure what to do next, so in a loud voice she said, "Follow that dog, *Luciana!*" Almost immediately a gust of wind caught the main sail with a snap and the little boat moved off in the direction of the receding black smudge that was George Ballchaser III.

The *Luciana* caught him quickly, its sails all puffed up with breeze, and as it pulled up alongside him, Lucy was able to lean over the side and lightly pat his head. George Ballchaser looked momentarily confused, then he was overjoyed to see her. She could tell from the special way he half-closed his eyes and his ears went flat and his tail started wagging under the water like a little propeller.

"You really are a silly dog, aren't you?" she said giggling. "Swimming all this way after a ball! Were you ever planning on giving up and paddling back to the beach? Or were you going to swim all the way around the world?"

George Ballchaser III decided not to respond to her jibe. He continued to paddle with quiet determination.

"I don't think I'm strong enough to lift you onto this boat and it is a loooooong way back to the beach for a not-so-little dog," she said, scratching her head. "Let me think."

Standing carefully and holding the mast, Lucy looked around. Close by she saw a very small island with a tiny beach.

"Go to that island, *Luciana*... please," she instructed the boat, thinking that it was probably time she treated the boat with some politeness instead of just barking commands. No need to talk like an 8 year old now that I'm nearly nine, she thought, quite pleased that she was already starting to think like a grown-up.

The *Luciana* headed toward the island.

"Follow me. And do try to keep up!" she shouted to George Ballchaser III as he paddled behind the boat.

❄ ❄ ❄

Sailing a boat was much easier than she'd ever imagined and ten minutes later they were both sitting on the small beach. George Ballchaser III looked rather exhausted—he was panting a lot and there was some seaweed tangled in his tail.

"Don't worry about the ball," she told him. "We'll get you another one just like it."

George Ballchaser III looked visibly relieved. He licked her hand.

"Eeeeeewwww," she said, "no licking!"

He kept licking but she didn't move her hand away or attempt to stop him.

"I was thinking, Georgie," she said, turning to George Ballchaser III after gazing at the sea for a bit. "It's still morning and we have quite a lot of the day left to fill with fun. If I was nine I'd probably ask the *Luciana* to take us home, but I'm only eight. I think I could ask her to take us on an adventure without getting into any trouble at all. Eight year olds aren't very responsible you know."

George Ballchaser III always agreed with everything Lucy said—even on rare occasions when she was being slightly rude or silly—and he agreed with her this time too. He loved adventures and was even less responsible than her, so this particular suggestion was a no-brainer in his book. She helped him up into the boat then climbed in herself, sitting where she thought the captain might sit on such a small craft, on its only seat.

"We're not ready to go home yet," she said to the *Luciana*, "so can you please take us on an adventure?" She added a "thank you very much" as an afterthought. A few moments later the sails puffed up with wind and the boat glided away from the small beach and out across the glassy sea. It tacked to starboard then sped toward the horizon.

3 | Birdland

Around about the time that Lucy was just starting to get bored with nothing to look at but water and with George Ballchaser III snoring loudly at her feet for what must have been a Very Long Time, some blue hills appeared on the horizon. She nudged him with her toe.

"Look, Georgie, we're going to arrive at our adventure quite soon," she said.

George Ballchaser III stood up and stretched, then shook himself. He yawned and blinked and wagged his tail. A few minutes later a beach came into view and a few minutes after that the *Luciana* came to a halt on the sand. Lucy tossed her shoes onto the sand then the pair jumped out into the shallows. She asked the boat to wait there for them, if it wouldn't be too much trouble please.

The beach was in a broad curving bay with golden sand and palm trees all along its fringes. Warm air rose up from the sand and shuffled around on a pleasant breeze. Behind the beach a grassy area with flax plants, cabbage trees and toetoes led to a sparse looking forest that ran right up the slopes into the blue hills. Those blue hills looked a lot greener up close.

The pair ambled up from the water's edge to where a tall gangly man, all limbs and angles, sat at a rather stuffy looking desk situated in the middle of the beach. Planted in the sand beside the desk was a sign that said "Customs". The sign had obviously taken some effort to make as several earlier versions with red lines through them sat in a pile of discarded attempts a few feet away. They included: Custons, Clusters, Cusstoms and Custard. On the desk were some pencils with chewed ends, a few blank pieces of paper and a stamp sitting face down on a green ink pad. There was a small sign neatly written on a plaque at the front of the desk that said 'OFFISHAL KAGU'.

The man was dressed in a suit made out of sleek blue-white feathers and he had a long red cardboard beak that was attached to his nose with an elastic string that went around the back of his head. A pair of round wire-rimmed glasses sat on his beak. He seemed to be in that half asleep, half awake state where your head falls forward and jerks back every so often.

"Ahem. Excuse me." said Lucy.

The birdman looked up with a startled expression, blinked at Lucy, then at George Ballchaser III, then he adjusted the feathers on his chest the way that important people who wear feathers always do.

"Passports please," he said in a practised tone.

"Sorry, what?" replied Lucy. Then she corrected herself remembering that she was almost nine. "Sorry, what please?"

"I didn't ask for your name, Miss Whatplease," the official said, "I asked for your passports."

"My name is Lucy," said Lucy. "And this is George Ballchaser the Third."

"Passports?" he said again, sounding a little tired from dealing with people who didn't just do what they were asked to do by important people, but did something annoying instead. He nodded in the direction of the *Luciana*. "That is your boat illegally parked on the beach, isn't it? I'll need to see your passports."

Lucy thought about this. The *Luciana* wasn't technically their boat, but it had come with them so technically maybe it was their boat.

"I'm sorry," she said, "we don't have passports. My friend here, George Ballchaser the Third, was chasing a ball in the water and we somehow ended up here thanks to the *Luciana* which isn't our boat but might be. Why are you dressed like a bird?" she asked.

"Dressed like a bird. Dressed like a bird! *I Am A Kagu*," he said. "An official one at that! Everyone is a bird in Birdland. We *only* have birds in Birdland," he added for emphasis, "although we might need to add 'bird-brains' to the list if you and your friend plan on staying. You will need a passport to go beyond this point, my little myna friend. Everyone has a passport here in Birdland."

"I'm nine," she said fibbing, hoping he'd get the hint and call her 'my good lady' or even 'young lady' instead of 'little myna friend'. Although, thinking through the combinations again, perhaps not 'young lady' either. When adults said that to you in that tone of voice, it still made it feel like you were a very small child.

"I really don't care how many names you have, Miss Whatplease, we need to sort out this passport debacle."

She pursed her lips. "Where can we get passports?" she inquired.

"By a lucky coincidence," he said, "you can get them here. I am the Passport Issuing Officer for Upper Birdland, Lower Birdland and the Passerine Peninsula. Let's see…you will need ten dollars…*each*…and a current photograph. Plus some form of proof that you are the species of bird you say you are."

"You're not a bird, that's a cardboard beak!" she exclaimed.

The eyes of the Passport Issuing Officer for Upper Birdland, Lower Birdland and the Passerine Peninsula went wide with a look of alarm and his jaw dropped. He shook his head.

"I am SO a bird!" he protested. He paused, looked at Lucy through slitted eyes then nodded his head wisely with a hmmmm sound.

"I see." he went on. "It's like that, is it? Alrighty then, five dollars each… and if they're crisp new bills instead of scruffy old ones I won't mention anything about your rude comments when I fill in the details on your passport."

"I don't have any money," she said, "and neither does Georgie," she added, noticing that he had turned his attention to George Ballchaser III as though the dog might be the one he should really be talking to.

He sighed. "Well what do you have to use for payment? Passports don't grow on trees, you know."

"We have a *Very Bouncy* white ball with red polkadots… um, had… it's out there," she said waving a hand at the sea behind them.

George Ballchaser III looked up at Lucy with sudden panic.

"Good enough," said the Passport Issuing Officer for Upper Birdland, Lower Birdland and the Passerine Peninsula.

"Don't worry, Georgie, I'll get you two more," she whispered to the dog.

He opened the top drawer of his desk and pulled out a pair of blank passports.

"Can you read?" he asked nervously.

"I read very well thank you," Lucy replied. "I mentioned I was nine didn't I?"

"Ah… hmmmm..." he said, fidgeting with his cardboard beak, "you can write too I suppose?"

"Of course I can," she said, beginning to wonder if she should have said she was ten or eleven.

"A recent rule change," he announced with a cough, "means that passports have to be made out in the handwriting of the bird who owns the passport. I'll dictate while you write."

He passed her one of the blank passports and licked the end of his pencil then gave her that as well. "On the first page, where it says: Name, write 'Sorry'—we don't need your surname on our passports, Miss Whatplease."

She wrote: Lucy, but he didn't notice.

"That next one, 'DoF', means 'Date of Fledge'," he said. "It's the date you took your first flight," he added, supposing that she might be a bit backward with things everybody knows.

She hesitated for a moment, then wrote: Nine.

"Now, under species write: 'Yellow spotted myna'"

This one had Lucy perplexed. She was wearing her pretty yellow dress so the 'yellow' part of his description was correct, but 'spotted myna' seemed a lot less accurate. On the other hand, she'd already written that she was nine when she was only *nearly* nine, so stretching the truth a little bit was probably okay on a passport. She wrote: Yellow Spotted Myna.

"Excellent!" he said. "Photo please?"

"I don't have one, not on me," she replied.

He rolled his eyes and sighed. "Draw one," he said, pointing, "in the top left square."

Lucy drew a flower—she liked drawing flowers—and proudly showed him.

"I don't see the likeness myself," he said, "but there you go. Your passport please?" he requested, holding out his hand.

She gave it to him and he opened it to the first blank page, pressed his stamp into the ink pad then stamped the page. A picture of a bird pecking at the ground appeared in green with 'Birdland' in bold letters above it and 'Top of the Pecking Order' below, as a motto. Then he wrote 'toaday onely' in wobbly letters underneath.

"I've given you a one day visitor's visa," he announced proudly, handing the passport back. He turned to George Ballchaser III and signalled for Lucy to give him the pencil.

"He doesn't write," she said, "or talk much."

George Ballchaser III barked.

"You see what I mean?" she said, touching her nose and whispering. "A bit limited, accident at birth."

The Passport Issuing Officer for Upper Birdland, Lower Birdland and the Passerine Peninsula glared at George Ballchaser III in a disapproving sort of way.

"He is actually a bird isn't he?"

"No," she said, "um…yes," she corrected herself. "He's a loon."

"Ah—well that explains why he can't write. Hmmmm." The official absent-mindedly moved the beak off his face to his forehead where it sat like a horn while he scratched his nose. His eyes went wide like saucers as he realised what he'd done and he placed it back on his nose immediately, then pretended to shuffle some papers in a storm of efficiency, whistling tunelessly to show that nothing unusual had just taken place.

"Admission denied!" he finally announced. "Now where did I put my *Deport Immediately* stamp?" He started shuffling through his desk drawers.

Lucy stared at the ground, not very pleased with this new turn of events, wondering what to do next. Then she smiled with a sudden inspiration. "Doesn't George Ballchaser III need a passport for you to stamp that in?"

"Yes, of course he does. Passport plea…" He stopped and looked at Lucy. "You'll need to make it for him."

Lucy took the other blank passport and wrote: George Ballchaser III esq.; Four; Loon; then drew another flower. She handed it to the Passport Issuing Officer for Upper Birdland, Lower Birdland and the Passerine Peninsula.

"As you may have noticed, I lost my deportation stamp," he said matter of factly, "so the loon can have a one-day visa too." He stamped the passport and wrote 'toady only'.

While this was going on, George Ballchaser III trotted down to the water's edge. The polkadot ball rolled in on a wave beside *Luciana*. He plucked it out of the water, trotted back to the desk and dropped it at Lucy's feet. She picked up the ball and placed it on the desk.

"Excellent!" he said, glancing furtively at her. "You're not expecting change are you?"

"Wouldn't dream of it," she responded.

He pulled a hankie out from under his breast feathers and wiped dog slobber off the ball, then dropped it into one of his lower drawers. "Enjoy your stay. Rookery, the main village in these parts, is that way," he said, pointing down the beach to the left, "and the Passerine Peninsula is down that way," he said, pointing to the right.

4 | Bananas

As Lucy and George Ballchaser III ambled along the beach toward the village they spied a banana grove. Hours had passed since her breakfast and even if it wasn't lunchtime yet, Lucy thought a banana might be just the thing for a late morning pick-me-up. They left the beach and wandered into the grove. The fruit that would have been within easy reach was gone, which was a bit unfair she decided, given that short people can't reach up as high as tall people, whereas tall people can bend down to reach as low as short people.

She was about to dazzle George Ballchaser III with this very interesting insight—in a most sympathetic way, of course, given his proximity to the ground and how urgently unfair this business of height must seem to him—when a husky feminine voice asked: "And what kind of bird walks with all four of its legs, hmmm?"

Lucy turned around in a full circle but didn't see anyone.

"Ahem, up here, little myna," said the voice.

Lucy looked up. What she had thought were two grey tree trunks were in fact legs.

Big legs. Elephant legs. They were attached to what appeared to be a very big elephant standing on her back pair, wearing a feather tutu and a feather hat.

"I can see that you are a myna of some sort, one of the yellow spotted ones is my guess, but that creature with you does not look like any bird I've ever seen," she said.

"His name is George Ballchaser the Third, and he's a loon," said Lucy. "I have his passport right here if you want to inspect it. Are you an elephant?"

"Bird…elephant bird," said the elephant bird.

"You look like an elephant to me."

"Rude little myna," said the elephant bird. "Have you ever actually seen an elephant bird before? Well?"

"No," admitted Lucy, "sorry."

"Elephant's walk on four legs, like your friend, the loon… and they lack feathers," said the elephant bird. "And for the record my name is Kamala," she added.

Lucy bit her lip and decided to change the subject. "Very pleased to meet you, Miss Kamala. My name is Lucy. You couldn't do me a favour could you please?" she enquired.

"That rather depends on the nature of the favour, doesn't it?" offered Kamala. "If, as a favour, you'd like me to eat lots of bananas and get all the sleep I want, then I'd say your request is very doable. If you'd like me to climb those blue hills in the distance with you on my back so that you can photograph butterflies for your mad Uncle Phillip's picture collection, I'd say the cost of spending your valuable breath to request something like that is way too high."

Lucy took a while to digest that. "More the first than the second," she eventually said.

"And yet you seem reluctant to specify your favour?" Kamala noted. "Not always a good sign… would you like me to stand on your friend, the loon, to make him easier to post home? Or perhaps you'd like me to sing?"

"I'm sure you're a very nice singer, Miss Kamala, and if you'd like to sing then we'd both like to hear you sing—wouldn't we, Georgie? But George Ballchaser the Third and I are having adventures today, so I don't need to post him anywhere unless I post myself with him."

George Ballchaser III barked loudly with appreciation.

"Do all loons quack like that?" asked Kamala, staring at him with a look of consternation.

"Just him," replied Lucy. "And actually, that favour I mentioned, I was just wondering if you could reach up and get me a banana—it's hours since I had my breakfast."

"Mmmhmmm," said Kamala. "You want me to reach up with my trunk... um, beak, I mean my beak... and twist off one of my bananas, and give it to you because... because... oh yes, because you are a peckish little myna. I suppose you aren't even troubled by what that might do to *Thurbinger's Law of Equilibrious Harmony?*"

Lucy shook her head with a frown. "What's *Thurbinger's Law of Equilibrious Harmony?*" she asked.

"Mynas are so unworldly," tut-tutted Kamala. "*Thurbinger's Law of Equilibrious Harmony* states that everything is in a delicate balance. When you upset that balance it all goes topsy-turvy. The whole shebang! Total catastrophe. Do you see what I mean?"

"Um...yes, I suppose," said Lucy, still a little uncertain about how this might relate to eating a banana.

"Soooo—stay with me on this little one—if I do you a favour, and you don't do me one... the whole universe becomes unbalanced," she paused for emphasis, "right? And that wouldn't be a good thing, would it?"

"Ah," said Lucy, "yes, I see now." She looked around the ground: "Is there something you'd like me to pick up for you?"

"Not really... but... there is one thing you could do..."

Lucy waited for her to go on but it looked like Kamala was falling asleep or else waiting for her to say something.

"What is it you'd like, Miss Kamala?" she prompted.

Kamala squeezed her eyes shut and said: "It's quite a lot to ask actually, but here goes... I have a very flexible elephant bird beak, as you may have noticed. It's a wonderful beak. It means I can scratch anywhere that itches, even the middle of my back. And elephant birds do get very itchy you see, itchiness is almost the curse of elephant birds, if you believe in such things as curses. But there's one place I can't reach that I really really want to scratch."

Lucy thought that this sounded like a very good riddle and started to imagine Kamala scratching herself all over with her beak to work out where she couldn't scratch, when Kamala continued.

"The tip of my beak," she sighed.

Lucy nodded her head thoughtfully. "This is a remarkable coincidence," she said slowly.

Kamala opened her eyes and stared at Lucy optimistically.

"I'm pretty good at scratching beaks," said Lucy, "but George Ballchaser the Third is an expert in that department!"

Kamala stared down at him. George Ballchaser III barked proudly.

"Would you like him to show you?" asked Lucy.

The elephant bird nodded her huge head.

"I suggest you sit down on your knees, including the two you don't use for walking," said Lucy, "and hold your beak out for him. Georgie will do the rest, he doesn't need any instructions."

Kamala did as Lucy suggested, clumping down so that her long beak was on the ground with its tip turned up for George Ballchaser III. George Ballchaser III began licking enthusiastically. Kamala's long eyelashes started to flutter and her giant ears shot out like sails, then she relaxed, closed her eyes with a look of bliss and let out a long happy sigh.

Ten minutes later the pair left the banana grove and turned towards Rookery. Lucy had a pretty sky-blue bag slung over her shoulder, a gift from Kamala, with three bananas and their passports tucked safely inside. She was eating the fourth banana. Kamala had tried to give them a whole bunch but Lucy couldn't even lift that many bananas.

"A pity you don't like bananas, Georgie," she said to her companion. "These are yummy ones."

George Ballchaser III gave a little bark which she took to mean that he could live with that disappointment so long as they were together having an adventure.

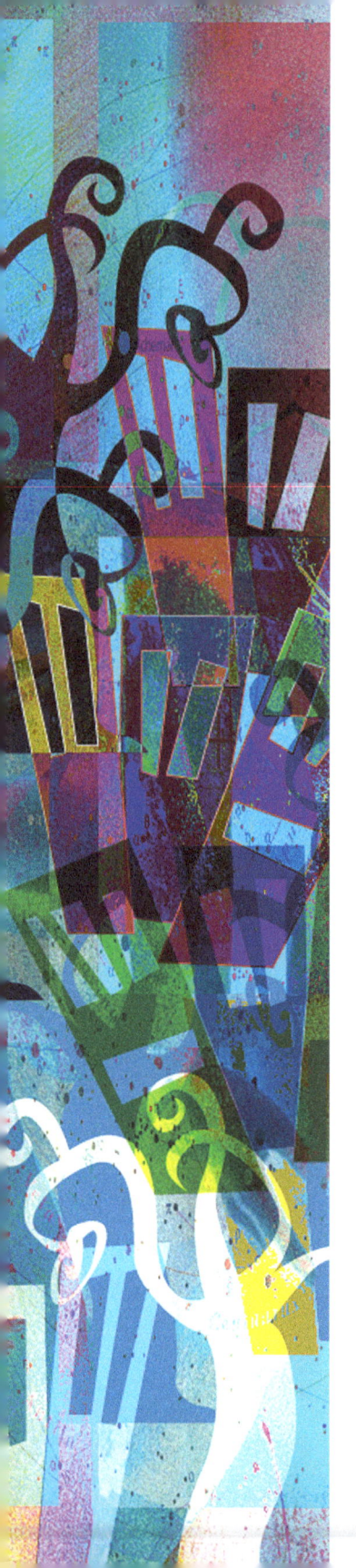

5 | Best in Show

Rookery was an eccentric town. It was filled with wonky buildings balanced on spindly legs, all set at improbable angles and supported by ropes and counterweights to stop them from falling over. The streets were cobbled with stones in every conceivable colour, jumbled together like the contents of a magpie's nest. Trees and bushes grew randomly, occasionally in the middle of the road or with their branches sticking through walls or into the windows of houses. Doors and windows were odd shapes and some houses had a wall or even two walls missing so you could see right through them. Water features that corresponded to oversized bird baths were prominent in most gardens.

Lucy and George Ballchaser III made their way through a confusion of alleyways and narrow streets, excusing themselves each time they wandered into someone's house—it was often hard to tell where a road ended and a living room started—but no one seemed especially offended by their intrusions.

They arrived at the town square to find that some sort of festival was in progress. Buntings and streamers dangled from poles and sagged between buildings. Gaily coloured flags hung from the windows of shops and dwellings clustered around the square. Townsfolk in eccentric bird costumes thronged the narrow streets that led in and out of the plaza and the square itself was a riot of noise and colour.

At the centre of the commotion, a man in a dinner jacket with a small wooden beak fastened to his nose, who vaguely resembled a penguin, appeared to be telling everyone what to do and how quickly to do it. Behind him a medium sized stage had been erected with a sign hanging over it that read: "Rara Avis". Under those words in small letters: "rare bird competishun". Next to the stage a number of odd-looking creatures milled around in a pen with large numbers painted on cards that were strung around their necks.

Lucy decided the penguin-man was far too busy to interrupt so she stood in front of an official looking man sitting next to him at a small desk concentrating on some sort of official looking form. This man resembled a barn owl. His downy hair was cut short into a severe widow's peak that pointed sharply down to the bridge of his nose. His close-cropped hairstyle went around his face in a broad circle that passed under his chin and mostly concealed his ears. Two flat ears crafted out of soft leather sat on top of his head and downy feathers were carefully plastered to the sides of his beakish nose. He wore a handsome cloak over his shoulders that fell down his back like a great pair of wings and his waistcoat was covered in speckled feathers.

"Excuse me!" she said at last, having waited a whole minute without any sign that he'd noticed her.

"Name and species?" he enquired in a monotone, not looking up.

"Lucy, Myna, Yellow Spotted," she replied as formally as she could.

"Entrant… Lucy… Myna… Yellow… Spotted…" he wrote on the form slowly, saying the words out loud. "And your name?" he paused. "Wait! Yellow spotted myna? There's nothing rare about mynas, even the spotted ones! Are you playing a prank, you cheeky passerine?"

He looked up at her.

"I'm sorry…" she said nervously, feeling that she'd done something wrong and that something might be her fault according to a set of rules she'd never heard of but had broken anyway.

He scrutinised her for a few moments, then looked down at George Ballchaser III, then raised an eyebrow.

"Ha!" he said. "Small misunderstanding, never mind. That fellow's name is what I meant, what's his name?" He pointed at the dog.

"George Ballchaser III, Loon," she said, relieved.

"I see," he said, "and you are Lucy, Myna, Yellow Spotted... yes, very good, very good."

He erased her name from the first column of his form and wrote it in the second, then wrote George Ballchaser III, Loon where her name had been.

"A loon? I've never seen a loon before. You're not a local then, Lucy, Myna, Yellow Spotted?"

"Just visiting for the day—we only have one day visas," said Lucy.

"Foreigners, hmmm, I'll need to make sure your passports are in order then," he said.

Lucy fished them out of her bag and handed them over. The owl-man inspected them and chuckled.

"Your visas are good for tomorrow too you know," he said

"But they say 'today only' don't they?" she asked, confused.

"Yes, tomorrow will be today, tomorrow," he said with a sly wink.

Lucy wondered if that was just how owls like to talk, but then she worked out what he meant and smiled back at him, attempting a wink of her own. She hadn't quite mastered good winking technique and tended to stretch her mouth open and screw up the whole side of her face which people found amusing—apart from George Ballchaser III who found it endearing.

"You'll go in as a hot favourite you know, especially if he can do some tricks. I don't think I've ever seen a bird with four legs before, that's as rare as it gets," chortled the owl-man.

"Win what?" asked Lucy, now very confused.

"The contest, the rare bird contest... you just entered your loon remember? Less than a minute ago."

"Did I?" she asked, feeling stupid.

"Right here," he said, pointing at his form. "Now put this number around the loon's neck before you forget that too and put him in the pen by the stage, we'll be starting in a minute. When his name gets called out, escort him onto the stage. You'll need a spade and bucket if you think he's going to soil himself."

"Georgie won't do anything like that," she said, screwing up her nose at the mere thought of having a dog with such a bad sense of timing. She knelt down beside George Ballchaser III and placed the number on him.

"Sorry, Georgie," she said, "looks like I entered you in a rare bird contest by mistake… but who knows? It might be fun."

George Ballchaser III licked her hand and stroked it with his head.

A tall woman dressed in a ball of pink flamingo feathers holding a small tortoise—which was covered in white downy feathers—glared at George Ballchaser III with an expression akin to horror. "What is that thing?" she demanded, pointing at the dog.

"He's not a thing, he's a loon," said Lucy defensively.

George Ballchaser III barked in agreement. The Flamingo-woman glared at him some more.

"Is it entered in the rare bird contest?" she asked at last, shaking her head.

"Yes," replied Lucy. "He's contestant eleven."

The woman continued to stare at George Ballchaser III the same way you might stare at your shoe after stepping in something you wish you hadn't. She had a flexible face and she contrived to wear several expressions at once, none of them pleasant.

"Come, Charles, this is a rigged contest," she said to her tortoise, turning on her heel and storming away.

"One less competitor for your loon," chuckled the owl-man. "Her turtle dove wouldn't have impressed the judges anyway."

They stood in the pen together with the other entrants and the competition got underway. The penguin-man waddled out onto the stage and waited impatiently for quiet from the crowd. He frowned at various people whom he deemed to be making too much noise, and scowled at others who might be thinking about opening their mouths. When he eventually spoke, it was with that peculiar booming voice that smallish people sometimes have.

"Rookerians, Passerians, migrating birds and seasonal visitors. Welcome to Rara Avis, our annual rare bird competition, the highlight of these Bird Week celebrations." He paused for the applause to die down then he continued. "I am Blatherhonk, your host, and today's distinguished panel of judges are Messrs Brightfeather, Saddleback and Tweet."

The judges, seated at a table on the stage, stood in turn to acknowledge a cheer from the audience. Brightfeather had the approximate appearance of a peacock, Saddleback looked like a raven with wattles, and Tweet a rather distinguished falcon.

"Our judges will award points to each of the entrants according to the following criteria," he continued. "First and foremost the bird in question must be rare. Last year, as you may remember, a fledgling myna entered her pet sparrow..." The crowd erupted in laughter. Blatherhonk acknowledged the response and went on. "But this year we have been more diligent so don't expect a replay.

"The next thing the judges look for is how precisely a competitor represents the ideal dimensions and qualities of its species. They consult such luminous authorities as Pugwiler's *Advanced Guide to Exotic Birds*, Trinket's *Bird Encyclopedia* and Fester's *Passeriformes*. Each judge is an expert ornithologist and Judge Tweet, as we all know, has written several important textbooks on microtonal dissonance in birdsong harmonics."

The falcon judge stood and took another bow as three or four people clapped unenthusiastically.

"Finally, if it comes to a tie on the points table, the judges will set a task for the competitors to determine the winner. Let us begin."

He took a card from his pocket and read from it: "Our first competitor is Gandhi, the Emperor Goose."

A medium sized goose was led out by a man who looked uncannily like a giant duck. The goose walked on black unjointed legs that wobbled alarmingly. Its long legs looked just like a pair of snakes with webbed slippers attached to their ends. The goose's head and neck looked snakish too, like a serpent that had been dipped in glue and rolled in feathers. Its body resembled a stitched bag covered in feathers that writhed and bulged in exactly the way a bag of snakes might. Some tail feathers poked out of its rear which hissed continuously. The audience applauded and there were many oohs and ahhs from people with a good view of the stage.

Judge Brightfeather began the inquisition. "Your goose is rather handsome but is he stable? He looks capable of collapsing on those trembling legs... why is that?"

"Ah," said the duck-man, "I can explain! Gandhi overexerted

himself earlier in the day. His exercise regime is strict and exuberant."

All three judges nodded slowly.

"That hissing sound," asked Judge Saddleback, "is your goose leaking swamp gas?"

"Naturally I regulate his diet but accidents do happen," responded the duck man. "Geese will be geese."

The judges all moved back in their chairs.

"Let's examine his excellent haunches shall we? A 360° twirl if you please so that we can marvel at his physique," requested Tweet.

The duck-man instructed his goose to pirouette. It made a loud hissing sound in its belly that Lucy could have sworn was a heated debate between various body parts, then the left leg turned clockwise and the right turned anticlockwise. The animal flopped to its belly with a dramatic thump whereupon a small viper exploded from Gandhi's rear like a sleek black missile that disappeared over the audience, finally lodging in the tail feathers of a large bird-of-paradise. The rest of the goose thrashed around in panic then rolled onto its back, legs and neck undulating in distress, hissing wildly.

Wasting no time, the duck man picked up his goose and leapt from the stage to howls of laughter from the audience. Lucy watched him push through the throng—which parted quickly around him—and disappear up a lane, his 'goose' hissing and writhing in his arms.

"Not a promising start," said Blatherhonk, with a nervous chuckle.

He called up the next contestant, a puffin named Dasher who had a bright red beak held in place with string. The puffin wore a vest with white plumage down the front and black plumage across his back. A pair of black wings were tacked to his arms. In all other respects he resembled an otter. He waddled onto the stage behind a woman who wore the markings and had the general demeanour of a kingfisher. The audience erupted into sustained applause for the puffin, who was very cute, and even Lucy clapped and cheered when he did a playful somersault as they exited the stage. The judges held up respective scorecards of 9, 8 and 7, an imposing tally.

One by one, each of the contestants took the stage and each was received warmly by the crowd, examined by the judges and scored appropriately. They included a kookaburra, a meadowlark, a kiwi that looked a lot like a hedgehog, a clumsy looking ostrich, a stunning blue cassowary and a very impressive shoebill stork that kept falling over. Dasher was still at the top of the leader board when George Ballchaser III was called up.

"Our final contestant," boomed Blatherhonk, "represents a species not found in these parts, George Ballchaser, Three, the loon!"

George Ballchaser III ambled out to the centre of the stage and a hush fell over the entire square. He wagged his tail and gave a happy little bark then plumped down on his hind quarters, his tail wagging on the stage behind him. All eyes were fixed on him and no one broke the silence. Lucy followed him onstage a little sheepishly and stood next to him. She grinned and waved at people who she thought looked nice but the quiet that had fallen upon the crowd was somewhat unnerving. She began to fidget then remembered the somersaulting puffin and thought that maybe it would help if George Ballchaser III did a trick or two to ease the tension.

"Sit, George Ballchaser the Third," she said loudly, then giggled because he was already sitting.

George Ballchaser III barked once to confirm his mission was accomplished, producing a round of gasps from all around the plaza.

Someone began clapping, and others joined in until the whole square was animated.

When the ruckus had died down, Tweet piped up: "I have never seen a four legged loon and only ever seen one other loon in my entire life, yet Plumy's *Avis Subterraneus*—the authority on the matter of ultra rare birds—stipulates that four legs are a quintessential feature of the extremely rare nocturnal loon... remarkable!"

Saddleback then drew the crowd's attention to George Ballchaser III's exotic black and white markings and his distinctive unique-to-loons vocalisations, then Brightfeather stood up and applauded, wiping a tear of gratitude from his eye. The plaza erupted with more applause. As the hubbub died down the judges held up their cards: 9, 9 and... 6! Brightfeather, overcome with emotion, was holding his 9 upside-down. Blatherhonk quickly tallied their scores and announced a two-way tie between George Ballchasher III, Loon, and Dasher, Puffin.

"Under rule 16, clause 21, sub clause 3b, we move now to a tie-breaker situation," said Blatherhonk. "Their companions will each be asked to nominate a trick that both of the entries must perform. We will select one of their tricks randomly, winner takes all."

He consulted with the Kingfisher-woman then with Lucy. He pulled a coin from his pocket, flipped it and continued; "Our chosen trick is a fish-eating contest. The contestants will have two minutes to eat a large bowl of herrings. The herrings will be counted before and after to determine a winner. Some herrings please?" he motioned to a stagehand.

A bucket of herrings and two bowls were brought to the stage. The puffin barked with glee and slapped his wings together.

"I hope you didn't have too much breakfast this morning, Georgie," Lucy whispered in his ear.

George Ballchaser III, loon, wagged his tail.

Blatherhonk counted out a dozen herrings into bowls and the owl-man came on stage to be the official timekeeper. On his order bowls were placed in front of the contestants and both began eating. The puffin, hampered by his wings and his beak which clearly got in the way, still managed nicely. He tossed them up and caught them in his mouth, swallowing each one whole and barking with delight.

George Ballchaser III was a less refined eater, planting his snout in the bowl and gobbling, but he was no less a lover of herrings than the puffin. Both contestants had finished their fish when the owl-man said stop. George Ballchaser III was licking his bowl.

"Another tie," announced Blatherhonk, looking perplexed. "Looks like we're down to the second and final trick—thankfully it is one that cannot be drawn. Can we clear a running track in front of the stage please and can the contestants prepare themselves at the start line. Oh, and does anyone have a ball on them?"

"I have one," shouted a man near the back of the crowd.

The Passport Issuing Officer for Upper Birdland, Lower Birdland and the Passerine Peninsula pushed his way to the front and presented Blatherhonk with a very bouncy white ball with red polkadots. He asked for a receipt and winked at Lucy.

"This is a ball retrieving trick," stated Blatherhonk. "I will toss the ball and the contestant that brings the ball back to me is the winner. Are you ready contestants?"

The puffin nodded. George Ballchaser III wagged. Blatherhonk tossed the ball down the running track.

George Ballchaser III flew like a rocket, a blur to the eyes of the delighted crowd, the puffin waddled uncomfortably, the way an otter walking on its hind legs might. He had only taken a few steps when George Ballchaser III screeched to a stop in front of him and dropped the ball at his feet. The puffin picked up the ball and waddled back to the start line, dropping the ball at Blatherhonk's feet. The crowd was silent.

"I hereby declare Dasher, Puffin, our official Rare Bird of the Year," announced Blatherhonk.

The Kingfisher woman squealed with delight and there was light applause in the audience spiced with murmuring. Tweet came down from the stage and whispered in Blatherhonk's ear. They talked for a moment then Blatherhonk cleared his throat again.

"The judges would also like to award a special one-off commendation this year. It is the 'Best Loon in Show' Certificate. This award recognises the special qualities of fairness and sociability that are a primary characteristic of loons (according to Plumy). This one-off prize goes to George Ballchaser, Three, Loon!"

The crowd erupted with cheering and applause. George Ballchaser III barked loudly and wagged his tail, as he always did when people applauded. Lucy was presented with an honorary degree in Ornithology from the University of Rookery, with Blatherhonk pointing out that it was the first time a myna had been so honoured. George Ballchaser III received lots of pats which was all he really wanted anyway.

An hour later as they strolled down the beach toward the *Luciana*, Lucy told George Ballchaser III that she was glad he gave the ball to the puffin.

"Being who you are matters a lot more than getting a prize for what you aren't, Georgie," she said. "And being George Ballchaser the Third's friend is the best prize of all."

George Ballchaser III gave a little bark which she took to mean it would probably be time for a nap soon, then they should think about finding him a new ball.

6 | Passerine Peninsula

Lucy woke up with a wet nose. George Ballchaser III was licking it with his big pink tongue.

"Really, George Ballchaser III—must you do that?" she giggled, giving her nose a wipe with the back of her hand.

She sat up and stretched, then looked around. The pair had been snoozing in the *Luciana* with George Ballchaser III pressed against Lucy's back for most of the time. While they slept the *Luciana* had sailed to a new location. The yacht was now resting on a sandy spur of the beach in a quiet cove, surrounded by lush tropical vegetation that came right down to the water's edge on either side.

Insects chirped and buzzed and the sun was still high in the sky as they leapt from the boat onto the speckled sand. There was birdsong too, the first evidence of real birds that they'd encountered on their journey.

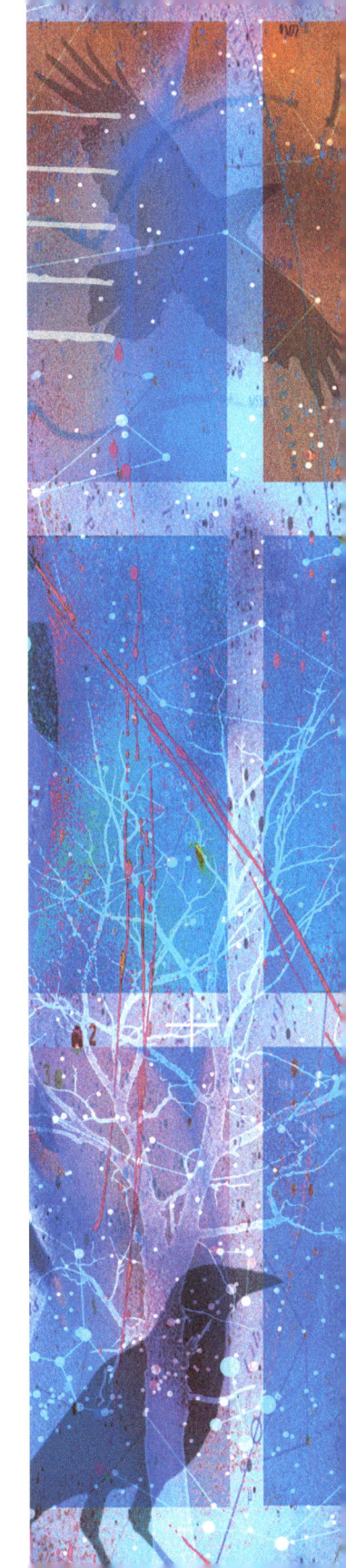

A few steps up the beach the gangly figure of the Passport Issuing Officer for Upper Birdland, Lower Birdland and the Passerine Peninsula was sleeping with his large feet on the desk. The desk sat under the dappled shade of a coconut palm. He was snoring loudly and leaning back in his chair which teetered precariously on its back legs, moving a few inches back and forth with each inhalation. His head was lolling in a horizontal position and his spindly cardboard beak stabbed at the sky like a small minaret.

Lucy wondered whether she should just let him sleep but was curious about where she was and which way to go to be somewhere fun so she stood in front of the desk and said: "Excuse me, Mr Kagu."

He woke up mid-snore making the sort of abrupt sound a pig would make if you waved something delicious under its nose. Removing his feet from the desk, then his glasses from his beak to clean them, he shook his head and said in a yawny voice: "Passports please?"

Lucy fished their passports out of her blue bag and placed them on the desk in front of him.

"Another loon!" he remarked with astonishment as he thumbed George Ballchaser III's passport, then looked up at Lucy and said, "oh, it's you two again… ha!"

He inspected their one day visas then pressed a little stamp into a light blue ink pad and then onto blank pages in both their passports. It said *Passerine Peninsula, home of the double syrinx* in a circle that looped around a small picture of a bird singing.

"Thank you," said Lucy. "What should we see here?" she asked.

"Ah," said the kagu-man. "This is the Passerine Peninsula—it's jam-packed with songbirds. Bird spotting is always popular here… and today we have an exhibition up at the flying school. You might enjoy that."

"Which way is that?" asked Lucy.

"That way," he said, vaguely wafting his hand toward a path leading into the jungle. "Before you leave though, I have a question… um, a problem that you might be able to help me solve."

"I'll help if I can," said Lucy, "but… well… even though I'm nine now, I don't really know all that much."

George Ballchaser III barked once to confirm that Lucy was telling the truth.

The kagu-man went into the third drawer of his desk and pulled out the ball with red polkadots. He placed it on the desk and stared intently at it.

"What does it do?" he asked, perplexed.

"Oh that's simple!" Lucy said. "It comes back to you."

"I don't understand?"

"Toss it away."

"Toss it away?" exclaimed the kagu-man. "But how does that work?"

"Try it and see… throw it as far as you can down the beach."

He stood up and walked a couple of paces from the desk with the ball in his hand. George Ballchaser III stared at him intently. Then he wound up like a baseball pitcher and tossed the ball as far as he could along the sandy part of the beach. George Ballchaser III exploded from a standing start and caught it aerially on second bounce. He raced back and dropped it at the Kagu-man's feet. The Kagu-man clapped his hands with delight and picked up the ball.

"Again?" he asked Lucy.

She nodded her head to say yes. He tossed it in the other direction. George Ballchaser III caught this one with a leap on first bounce. The kagu-man clapped some more, clearly excited. The pair played fetch as Lucy settled down on the sand and ate a banana. She offered one to the kagu-man between throws, which he accepted, pulling out a wastepaper basket from under his desk for the skins.

"What's your name Mr Kagu?" she asked him.

"My name?" he asked, surprised. "No one ever uses my name. Mostly they say 'sir', or 'officer', or 'you there'."

"You do have a name though, don't you?"

"Oh yes, it's on my passport, just a moment."

He fished his passport out of his wing pocket, opened it and looked surprised.

"Well—I'll be…" he said. "Pierrot, my name's Pierrot. You know I'd quite forgotten!"

"That's a lovely name! It's very nice to meet you properly, Mr Pierrot," said Lucy.

Pierrot smiled broadly so that from side-on his lips disappeared behind the cardboard beak. "And you two are by far the nicest tourists this office has processed in a long while," he said. He tossed the ball a few more times.

"I could show you the way to the aerodrome if you'd like some company," he offered.

"We'd like that a lot wouldn't we, Georgie?"

George Ballchaser III barked once, staring intently at the ball in Pierrot's hand. Lucy thought that perhaps he had mistaken the offer for "I could throw the ball all the way to the aerodrome if you'd like?" but she decided not to explain that mistake to George Ballchaser III.

Pierrot dropped the ball into a pocket with a smile. George Ballchaser III stared intently at the pocket.

He took off his spectacles and polished them on his blue-white feather suit then placed them back on his beak. Then he took a key from a breast pocket and locked each of the drawers in turn and, finally satisfied that his desk was in order, told the pair to follow him. He struck out with awkward lanky strides toward the path leading away from the beach. Lucy followed a few steps behind jumping from footprint to footprint. George Ballchaser III barked twice at the *Luciana*, then trotted after them.

The track wound through a dense thicket of tropical vegetation: palms, banyans, figs, jackfruit, plantain, bamboo, and an assortment of vines and creepers. The birdsong surrounding them got louder, but Lucy still couldn't see any movement in the treetops that might indicate birds. Pierrot held up his hand and they stopped abruptly.

"Look up there," he said pointing, "A Spix's Macaw!"

Lucy followed his finger into the upper branches of a nearby sycamore fig. A gibbon wrapped in a blue feather cloak with a long blue tail and a bright white hood sat on one of the boughs turning the crank of some sort of music box. The box produced a steady stream of parrot chatter and squarks.

"Good day to you, Macaw!" Pierrot called up to the bird.

"Who's a pretty boy, rarrrk," said the macaw-gibbon, adjusting his handsome curling plywood beak.

"The birds here are so colourful, aren't they?" Pierrot said to Lucy. "It's a tropical thing I suppose."

Lucy giggled and waved to the Macaw who winked back.

They resumed their trek and Lucy started to see lots of monkeys dressed as birds in the surrounding branches creating a loud din of bird chatter with their music boxes. George Ballchaser III barked in a friendly way at one or two of them and wagged his tail approvingly.

The track snaked around some giant banyan trees then took them through the middle of a swamp which was crisscrossed by a series of small bridges. There was a rotten-egg smell emanating from the brackish waters and even George Ballchaser III—normally pretty keen on strong odours—looked less than impressed.

Lucy paused on the biggest bridge to examine three large inverted funnels made out of banana leaves that hung, secured by vines, above a bubbling black pool. Attached to the narrow tops of these funnels, three pipes hollowed out of fatter vines threaded through some overhanging branches before arriving at a table placed in the middle of a grassy knoll. The pipes attached to a set of nozzled valves that were bolted onto the table top. A very serious looking orangutan in pink feathers stood in front of the table filling balloons with gas from the pipes. He tied each inflated balloon to a rock and moved it to a cart where the balloons strained on their taut strings in colourful clusters.

Lucy wanted to approach the orangutan and ask what the balloons were for but Pierrot barely even glanced in the pink orangutan's direction and Lucy was scurrying to keep up with him anyway. A few minutes beyond the swamp, they came to a clearing with a signpost that read "PP Skool of Eerienautix" at the top, "Aerodrome" in official looking hand-writing below that, and in scrawly handwriting further down, "TOADY: Exibishun".

"We're here," announced Pierrot with a broad smile, "and it looks like the exhibition is just getting started."

7 | Airborne

Pierrot, Lucy and George Ballchaser III made their way to where a small crowd of feathered creatures were gathered on the landing strip. It was a very official looking aerodrome with a control tower that teetered on spindly legs, some hangers that contained various odd-shaped contraptions, and a landing strip with stripes, circles, dotted lines, arrows and other symbols painted on it.

The crowd comprised an eccentric assortment of birds. In the centre, a woman wearing the elegant black and white plumage of a royal albatross was talking to a baboon who had the markings and oily feathers of a shag and the pair were inspecting a hippo decked out in the long loose hairy feathers of an emu.

A ground crew of orangutans—who had a passing resemblance to canaries in yellow mechanics' overalls—were attaching balloons to the emu, arguing over which size and colour balloon to fasten where. She had a heavy leather strap under her armpits and another around her bulging waist.

On attaching the 26th balloon to the strap around the emu's midriff, she became buoyant and started to wobble 30 cms above the ground. There was a small amount of applause from the crowd, mingled with high fives and excited wooting from the ground crew.

The canaries set about stabilising her: attaching a fin to her tail and large banana leaf paddles to her limbs. The albatross inspected her, noting important things on a clipboard and checking the various fastenings in a very official way. The shag wiped her goggles and offered last minute advice, then the ground crew nudged her into the starting circle.

Finally, the albatross turned to the crowd. "Our first demonstration today is called wing-sailing," she said. "Jumela will demonstrate flying with the addition of moveable sails attached to her wings and feet."

There was a ripple of applause. The albatross continued: "As you all know, these are timed demonstrations where the flyer is required to remain airborne from the starting circle down to the red marker; to execute a turn which establishes that she is actually flying and not drifting hither and thither on the breeze; and to make her way back to the starting circle. We time her downwind and upwind speeds, plus her overall return-trip duration."

She glanced around the gathering, pausing to smile at Lucy who waved back, then continued. "The records for these feats are still held by Zephyr, Wood Pigeon, with 'Giant Sail' for the downwind leg, although the jury is still arguing over that record as no turn was ever executed and no one has actually seen or heard of Zephyr in the two months since she sailed over yonder trees. Avril, Pelican with 'Gondola' holds upwind and return records. Those times are listed at 26.343 seconds downwind; 1 minute, 22.2 seconds upwind; and 2 minutes, 18.03 return. Let's see if Jumela can break any of these records, shall we?"

The crowd turned their attention to the hovering emu who looked very serious in her goggles and leather hat. Two of the canaries produced stop watches and one headed down to the red marker while a third pulled out a starter's gun. Each held up a wing when they were ready to proceed. Jumela gave the emu/hippo equivalent of holding up a thumb. The albatross nodded to the starter who fired the gun and Jumela started flapping her limbs in a kind of random breast stroke arrangement.

She didn't move.

She flapped strenuously for a whole minute but failed to go forward even an inch. Finally the shag pulled out a whistle, shook it to remove any traces of spittle, and started to blow in short bursts to indicate when to flap her sails. Jumela got into a more organised rhythm and started to nudge forward in tiny jumps. The crowd applauded and murmured approvingly. Lucy and Pierrot clapped and George Ballchaser III barked a few times excitedly.

Although it was clear no new records were going to be set with Jumela's attempt, the spectacle of such a large animal swimming ponderously across the landing strip was really quite fabulous and a couple of excited mynas skipped along beside her, one hanging streamers from the rudder attached to Jumela's tail.

While this was going on, a second flying demonstration was being prepared. A weasel bedecked in the plumage of a kingfisher hovered from a single blue balloon attached by a string to his waist. He was holding a second smaller red balloon by its neck under his belly. This made him rather too buoyant and a second kingfisher-weasel stood below him holding a guy-rope to stop the hovering kingfisher from floating off. The ground crew guided him into the starting circle where he awaited inspection from the albatross.

The albatross studied all the fastenings, wriggled the kingfisher's rudder, and made several notes on her clipboard. As Jumela's time seemed not to matter any more, all the stopwatches were reset. The albatross turned back to the audience.

"Next," she said, reading from the clipboard, "is Pottle, Kingfisher, with 'Jet Engine'. Pottle's wingman is Prattle, who you'll see working the guy-ropes."

There was a round of applause as Prattle bowed and both Pottle and Prattle gave the thumbs up. A nod from the albatross and the starter's gun went off again.

Pottle released some swamp gas from the red balloon—which gave off a raspberry sound and a foul smell—and swiftly took off in the direction of the marker with Prattle running to keep up.

Pottle narrowly avoided crashing into the back of Jumela—who was still swimming methodically along the landing strip—by executing a deft barrel-roll, but in the process, released more gas than intended and accelerated unexpectedly. Prattle yelped, thrown off his stride by the additional burst of speed and the guy-ropes came loose in his hands.

He leapt up and caught them again, then stumbled and fell flat on his face, tangled in the guy-ropes. Pottle, attached to the other end of the ropes, did a slow motion nosedive into the runway, saved from injury only by bouncing on the balloon he was grasping to his chest. It exploded, releasing a dreadful stench, and he bounced comically along the runway stopping an inch short of the red marker.

Jumela paddled into the miasma of swamp gas from the burst balloon. She started coughing and flailing wildly, coming to a dead stop and turning green. Her shag companion signalled to the ground crew for assistance. It was clear that Jumela had no further interest in flying. The ground crew untied one of her balloons and she floated serenely to the ground.

The albatross stared at all the commotion on the runway with a frown. She consulted her clipboard and searched around the crowd, settling with a smile on Lucy and George Ballchaser III. She waddled up to them and asked: "Are you ready."

"No... um yes... ready for what, please?" Lucy asked.

"You are a myna, aren't you?"

"Yes," replied Lucy.

"And your friend here is B. Loon?"

"Yes..um, no... G. B. 3. Loon, actually."

"Close enough. I have you listed as the next demonstration."

Lucy thought hard about this. Maybe the albatross had confused her with another myna and loon team, but that seemed unlikely. Perhaps, she concluded, she'd entered them in the air show and just forgotten—that seemed much more like the sort of thing she'd do.

"So which of you is flying?" asked the albatross.

Lucy looked at George Ballchaser III and decided he was much more of a running loon than a flying one. "Me," she said, "I'm Lucy, Myna, Yellow Spotted. George Ballchaser III, Loon, is my Wingman and Mr Pierrot, Kagu, is my Tactician," she said, proud to have thought of a job for Pierrot even though she had no idea at all what a tactician might be. Pierrot beamed a big smile at her.

"Excellent," said the albatross, noting down the details. "And what do you call your style of flying?"

"Good Boy," she replied.

The albatross smiled and winked at Pierrot in a *that's mynas for you* sort of way, then she escorted the three to the ground crew and instructed them to prepare Lucy for her flight demonstration. Lucy asked for a long string and as many red balloons as might be needed to lift her off the ground. The string was tied to George Ballchaser III's collar and attached at the other end to the yellow belt on Lucy's dress. Four red balloons were also attached to her belt and she found herself hovering horizontally a metre off the ground.

"Stand by me when the starter's gun goes off," she said to Pierrot, then whispered secret instructions in his ear.

Pierrot yelped and clapped his hands with excitement.

Lucy was moved to the starting circle by the ground crew where she hung in the air waving to the small crowd. The albatross inspected her balloon fastenings and the string that ran between Lucy and George Ballchaser III.

"Our next demonstration is called 'Good Boy'," said the albatross, addressing the crowd with a wry smile. Some of the mynas in the crowd giggled. "As our aviatrix is only a myna, I hope you can all give her a round of applause no matter how she does."

"Timekeepers to your stations please." She turned back to the audience. "Lucy, Myna, Yellow Spotted, is our flyer. George Ballchaser III, Loon, is her wingman, and Mr Pierrot, Kagu, is her tactician."

The crowd clapped and Pierrot took a bow. He extracted the polkadotted ball from his wing pocket and gave the thumbs up. Lucy gave a thumbs up and George Ballchaser III barked once. The albatross nodded and the starter gun went off.

Pierrot leaned back and tossed the ball out past the red marker. George Ballchaser III flew after it in top gear with Lucy pulled after him at the end of the string. He screeched to a stop, gathered up the ball, and turned, which made Lucy snap through her own turn just past the red marker. George Ballchaser III raced back to Pierrot and dropped the ball at his feet. Lucy flew back to the starter circle in his wake, a giggling blur of yellow dress, red balloons and straw coloured hair.

The crowd erupted in applause and the timekeepers ran together to confer then passed their stopwatches to the albatross who shook her head and noted down the times. Lucy was lowered to the ground still giggling and her balloons were removed.

"Passerines, avians, fledglings and chicks," the albatross announced. "We have three new records... amazing! Downwind: 3.22 seconds; upwind: 2.45 seconds and 5.67 seconds return. That's a massive 23.123 seconds off the downwind record, 1 minute, 19.75 off the upwind and a whopping 2 minutes, 12.36 off the return record!" She shook her head some more.

Birds of all sorts of feathers flocked around Lucy, George Ballchaser III and Pierrot to congratulate them. The ground crew lifted Lucy onto their shoulders with wooting and other un-bird-like (but quite orangutan-like) sounds and carried her through the crowd.

Lucy was returned to the ground and the albatross joined the three of them at the centre of the throng. The albatross made some "ahem" and "if you please" sounds and the crowd fell silent.

"In recognition of this outstanding feat of flying," she intoned gravely, "the Passerine Peninsula School of Aeronautics presents Lucy, Myna, Yellow Spotted; George Ballchaser III, Loon; and Mr Pierrot, Kagu with Gold Wings—our highest honour!"

She opened a small case that one of the ground crew had just handed her and took out three small gold brooches shaped like wings, attaching one to Lucy's dress, one to Pierrot's feather jacket, and clipping the third to George Ballchaser III's collar. He wagged excitedly as the crowd erupted with applause again.

"Gold wings denote special achievement in aeronatics and carry the official title, 'Flying Instructor'," said the albatross.

They were engulfed by wellwishers again and it took quite a long time before the three of them were able to shake hands with everyone and extract themselves from the excited throng.

As they made their way toward the track leading to the beach, a myna in a pink dress, a bit younger than Lucy, ran up to her and held out a yellow balloon as a gift.

"B'loon," said the little myna.

Lucy beamed a big smile at her and accepted the balloon. She unclipped her golden brooch and gave it to the myna who squealed with delight, racing back to her parents to show them her prize. Pierrot, George Ballchaser III and Lucy headed off down the track.

Twenty minutes later they were back on the beach.

"Are you sure that balloon was a good swap for your gold wings, little myna?" asked Pierrot. He'd clearly been mulling over the exchange, being somewhat elated with his own set of wings.

"Oh yes," said Lucy. "Quite sure."

He thought about it some more. "You are a very smart little myna, aren't you?"

"I'm almost nine," said Lucy, with pride.

George Ballchaser III barked in agreement.

Pierrot pulled the ball out of his pocket and looked at it. "I suppose," he said, "this ball doesn't really work all that well unless there's a loon about, does it?"

"I've never really played fetch without Georgie," confessed Lucy. "Although it did come back to us once when we threw it in the sea."

He nodded and handed the ball to Lucy. "I think you two should have it," he said.

"But what about *Thurbinger's Law of Equilibrious Harmony?*" she asked. "I don't have anything to give you?"

"Not so," replied Pierrot, holding up a dismissive hand. "I now have the title Flying Instructor and I have Gold Wings, all thanks to you and George Ballchaser III."

Lucy smiled and thanked him. "Georgie is very keen on this ball, but that's loons for you," she said, happy that she'd slipped another adult expression into the conversation, which must be something nine-year-olds do all the time she'd already decided.

She skipped down to the *Luciana* and tied B'loon to the prow which made the yacht look very jaunty indeed. Then she returned to Pierrot's desk and thanked him for the excellent adventure. George Ballchaser III thanked him for the ball with a big elastic doggy smile and a wag, and after their farewells, the pair retired to the yacht.

Lucy felt drowsy so she stretched out on the deck of the craft with a big yawn and George Ballchaser III snuggled up next to her because that was the most satisfying way he could imagine to spend sleepy time with his best friend.

As the pair drifted off to sleep, the *Luciana* slipped back out to sea.

book two

Falde

1 | Arrival

She could feel grainy, sandy pressure on her back and the tingle of a watery sun on her face. An orange blackness inside her eyelids was the sort where descending luminescent dots jump back to the top when they reach the bottom of your eyes.

She could hear the sea—waves rattling small shells as they spent themselves against the sand. There was an aroma too, of flowers, tropical sweetness threading in and out of seaweed and brine.

After a while the beach-rhythm was disturbed by tuneless whistling and crisp footsteps, growing closer and louder. A shadow fell across her orange eyelid sky. She dragged her eyes open. A man's face hovered, rim lit, his head outlined in a sun halo. He wore a blue-white bird costume and had a long red cardboard beak topped with wire-rimmed glasses. He looked perplexed. She smiled and closed her eyes again.

Some time later she became aware of her surroundings again but could find none of her memories, only new impressions: a beach; being wrapped in a blanket and transported in a squeaky wooden barrow; being winched into a treehouse; an owl-like man with a stethoscope at her bed—a nest of twigs and leaves.

She could hear voices in the house below her.

※ ※ ※

"Without plumage, I can't tell you what sort of bird she is."

Saddleback shrugged his shoulders and raised his brow with a 'what else can I say—I'm a renowned ornithologist and I don't have the slightest clue' expression. He adjusted his tail feathers to make the stool he was perched on more comfortable.

"Saddleback's right. We have little choice but to wait for the patient to regain her wits, then ask her directly," added Dr Banggai-Scops.

"I see." Pierrot scratched his chin. "I think… ahem…," he lowered his voice and glanced furtively at the other two. "I have a theory… I think it's *her!*" he said quietly. *"The myna,"* he added in a whisper.

"Quite large for a myna," said Saddleback.

Banggai-Scops nodded sagely.

"Not a myna—THE myna! *The Yellow Spotted!*" he turned his back to the other two, moved his cardboard beak to his forehead and scratched his nose absentmindedly, then replaced it in the middle of his face. He turned back. They were both staring at him.

"Impossible," said Banggai-Scops. "Mynas don't grow that big."

"A flotsam bird," intoned Saddleback in his most scholarly voice. "Most likely she fell from her nest in yesterday's storm. My *educated* guess is her perch was hanging over water and she was swept out to sea. Perhaps the violence of the storm and the tumble of the ocean account for her missing plumage?" He smiled and nodded, increasingly pleased with his theory as he replayed the scene in his head.

"I don't think… no, she's too big… not the myna, Pierrot" Banggai-Scops added gently.

"But I have the myna's passport," said Pierrot, "she gave it to me for safe keeping—'just in case'. Her picture…the likeness… it's… see for yourselves."

He pulled the passport from his wing pocket and handed it to Saddleback who stared at the picture and pursed his beak, passing it to Banggai-Scops.

The passport picture was a simple hand drawn flower.

"Hmmm. It's an excellent likeness," said Banggai-Scops in a serious tone. "But if it is her, what's this growth spurt about? And where is her companion, the loon?"

"I would very much like to talk to the loon," added Saddleback wistfully.

"Loon," said the young woman. She stood in the doorway, naked.

"Plumage!" erupted Saddleback in a panic, flapping his wings.

Pierrot leapt to his feet and led her into a side room. He handed her his own nightgown—a long plain white shirt with an embossed feather motif—with out-stretched arms, eyes averted, prompting her to put it on quickly. She complied and he led her back into the study.

"Ah. The patient is awake," intoned Banggai-Scops in his cheerfully commanding medical voice.

"This is Lucy Whatplease," announced Pierrot, looking sideways at her to see how she'd respond to him using the myna's name.

Saddleback was still fanning himself. "We really must find you some proper plumage… young *myna*, is it?"

She smiled and shrugged.

"Ah, yes, that!" said Pierrot. "Now that you're awake, we have some questions, if you don't mind. Would that be all right?"

The young woman he'd introduced as Lucy Whatplease turned to Pierrot. "Questions," she said, flatly.

"Yes. You were last here—by the reckoning of Nester's Avian Calendar—one year, fifty one weeks and a day and a half ago…"

Pierrot paused as it occurred to him that his memory of these events was a little obsessively over-precise, almost as though he'd been counting the days. His eyes darted nervously toward his companions and he corrected himself, "Well approximately, give or take a day or so."

He coughed and turned to his guests with an unprompted aside. "My timekeeping is up there with the cuckoos. Always has been. Precise to a fault. A kagu thing…" His explanation petered out with a toothy smile and he turned back to the woman. "Ahem. Is that your memory too, young myna?"

"Memory," she said, shaking her head. She held out her hands in an empty gesture.

"Oh my!" said Banggai-Scops. "Avian amnesia. Total." He shook his head. "Worst case I've seen."

He looked at Saddleback who stared back with a raised eyebrow. "Worst of the *two* cases I've seen." He glanced at Pierrot and back at Saddleback. "Two including this one," he added, "the other lasted a few minutes."

"Perhaps you can prompt Miss Whatplease's memory with some trinket or bauble she'll recognise, Pierrot?" suggested Saddleback.

"Mynas are fascinated by shiny things."

"YES!" Pierrot exclaimed. "Just the thing!" He leapt into action, disappearing down the hallway, returning with a small box. He opened it and pulled out a gold wing badge which he handed to her. She squealed with delight.

"Ha!" said Pierrot, "She's seen this before. Thought so! You recognise these wings don't you, young myna?"

"Wings," she repeated back to him, turning them over in her fingers.

"Yes. I got mine as your tactician when we broke all the records with your 'Good Boy' flight system. And our friend the loon got one too as your wingman. And you gave yours to another myna in exchange for a yellow balloon. You remember it all don't you, Lucy?"

He turned. "All three of us are flight instructors," he said proudly to Saddleback and Banggai-Scops.

"Balloon," she said.

"Excellent!" said Pierrot. "Memory's back. Worked a treat. Not surprised. Special day that was. Historic really. One of those 'where-were-you-on-that-day' sort of days." He puffed up his chest feathers and half closed his eyes.

"Sterling!" said Saddleback. "And timely too! Next week is our annual Loon Festival, named in honour of her friend. Bring her to Rookery, Pierrot. Find suitable plumage and restore her beak and she can be the guest of honour on the GBIII float in the parade."

"Ha!" he replied. "Who knows? Now that her memory's restored, maybe we can find the loon too and entice him to come along!"

Saddleback clapped his wings with a coo. "Oh that would be splendid! Just splendid!" he exclaimed.

"Don't rush the patient though," cautioned Banggai-Scops. "Memory is a tricky business, she might not have *all of it* back."

She smiled at Banggai-Scops. "All of it," she said, enigmatically.

2 | Plumage

"Bit big for a myna, isn't she? Never seen a myna even half as big as that!"

Mr Dickenshaw, Tailer, was a plump, wry-humoured fellow with a narrow bristling pelt of dark hair extending in a V from the bridge of his beaky nose, arching above his eyes and disappearing behind his ears. His hair was slicked back in the style of a parrot, a sulphur tinted crest bouncing colourfully on his crown.

Lucy Whatplease stood by a clothes rack running her fingers over feather cloaks and the various downy fabrics displayed on the hangers, delighted with their textures. Pierrot stood at the counter of Dickenshaw's Plumage discussing her outfitting with the store's proprietors.

"On the large size, yes," Pierrot replied wearily.

"You're certain she's a myna?" inquired Mrs Dickenshaw, whose markings and colourings indicated a smaller, dowdier female of the same sulphur crested parrot species.

"Quite certain," said Pierrot, holding up a hand. "Her species has been confirmed by none other than our scholarly friend, Professor Saddleback." He paused for emphasis, then continued. "And anyway, I've known her for years—two in fact—

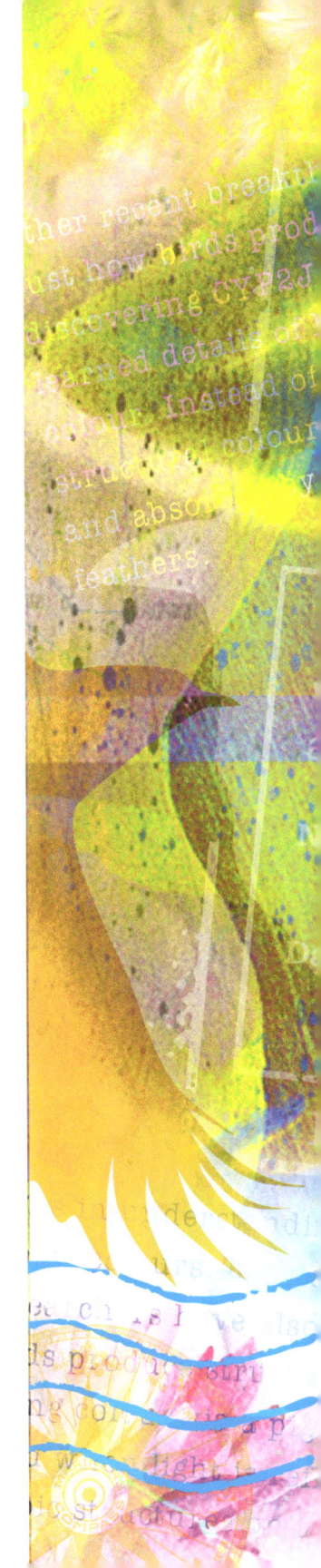

and I assure you she's a very special yellow spotted myna."

"Hmmm. The yellow spotted myna is one of the smallest members of a genus renowned for their lack of stature," opined Mr Dickenshaw, his skepticism firmly intact. "We have yellow spotted myna plumage in small and very small here, nothing at all in gigantic, I'm afraid."

"She's hardly gigantic," argued Pierrot. "No taller than you or I. I'm not seeing an ostrich or an emu," he said, glancing toward her.

"Well, I'm a very big parrot," responded Mr Dickenshaw, "and you're at the extreme end of the curved beak for a kagu," he added.

Mrs Dickenshaw nodded her agreement. "Precisely Mr Dickenshaw," she added. "Nothing in the back room either for a gargantuan myna."

Pierrot removed his spectacles to wipe them on a square of feathercloth and sighed. He replaced them on his beak. "Perhaps you have something in yellow for a similar species of bird and we can add the spots? Or something in white that we can dye yellow?"

"We have a white peacock?" proffered Mrs Dickenshaw.

"Tail's all wrong," said Mr Dickenshaw, jumping on her suggestion, "and the crest… flashy, exotic, nothing remotely like a common or garden myna."

"Peacock's a very big bird though," she offered in her defence, nodding her beak towards Lucy to indicate the young woman's unlikely dimensions.

Mr Dickenshaw stared at his wife critically.

"Not your best work, Mrs Dickenshaw. Appalling really. Why not an elephant bird or a cassowary or a rhea?" he said, "if size is the only criteria we use at Dickenshaw Plumage to evaluate our customer's needs."

"Now now!" said Pierrot, holding up a hand. "Let's not squabble like pa…" He bit his lip.

"Like pa…?" enquired Mrs Dickenshaw.

"Parakeets!" he said nervously. "Your quarrelsome *distant* relatives. Reputation you know." He tapped the side of his beak in an unconvincing conspiratorial gesture.

She peered at him through slitted eyes and hrmphed.

"How about a kagu?" suggested Mr Dickenshaw somewhat smugly. "That's a smallish, whitish bird we keep outsized plumage for," he said pointedly.

Pierrot opened his mouth to protest, then caught himself. "A kagu will do splendidly," he said. "We'll take two."

❃ ❃ ❃

Pierrot sprinkled a pouch of yellow dye into the wooden bucket—its watery contents turned vivid yellow. "I have an idea for the white spots," he said to his companion, stroking his beak.

"Spots?" she asked, quizzically.

"Yes, you know, yellow *spotted* myna."

"Myna?"

"You really don't remember much, do you little myna?" he said, glancing up from the Kagu plumage beside the bucket.

"I don't remember anything before yesterday, Pierrot," she said, surprising him with her first proper sentence that wasn't an echo of what had just been said to her.

He was tempted to recount in detail their adventures with George Ballchaser III in Rookery and on the Passerine Peninsula, but refrained. Instead he asked, "but… you remembered our golden wings, didn't you?"

She smiled broadly and shrugged.

"Why are you wearing a cardboard beak?" she asked.

His eyes went wide. "You asked me that the first time we met! Terribly rude." He stroked his beak. "At least that proves it's you and not a warbler or a sparrow pretending to be you, as if further proof were actually needed," he muttered. "I forgave you last time because young myna's have a reputation for rude chatter."

He stirred the dye. "And this time you've lost your manners with your memory so I'll make another exception."

She arched an eyebrow, waiting for a proper answer that wasn't just a complaint about her manners.

"We're all birds little myna," he explained. "Obviously! This is Birdland."

She reached across and pulled his beak a few centimetres off his face, stretching the elastic that held it in place. Pierrot squawked with alarm, flapping his arms. She let it go and it snapped back over his nose.

He was clearly shaken. "Do NOT do that ever again! Height of rudeness. Very disagreeable." He probed his beak gingerly and made a small adjustment, then retrieved the spectacles that had jumped off his face. He brushed sand off them and placed them back on his beak.

"For your information, what you just did is classified under Birdlaw as Avian Assault, First Degree. You don't want to end up in a cage do you?" he warned, wagging a finger.

"I'm sorry," she said with a mischievous glint in her eyes, obviously not all that sorry. "I was just trying to make a point... about the beak."

"Oh?" he said, "and that point would be?"

"Better if you work it out yourself, Pierrot," she said, smiling.

Pierrot had no idea at all what she wanted him to be working out but he knew whatever it was, it was bound to involve myna logic, which is to say, none at all. He turned back to his bucket and dipped a feather into the dye to test its colour.

"Why are there three beds in your house when you live alone? Do you often rescue castaways?" she asked.

"No," said Pierrot, "you're the first. There's my summer nest, where you're roosting. Then there's the winter nest, which has extra straw, feathers and moss. That's where I've been roosting the last couple of days. It's rather hot in my winter nest at this time of year," he said, trying not to sound like he was complaining.

"So why aren't we sharing the summer nest?" she queried.

He looked at her like she'd just hatched. "We're not the same species," he said, adding, "you'd have to be cuckoo to do that."

He was happy with the test-feather so he plunged the whole kagu outfit into the bucket. "And then there's the family nest. That's for my chicks when I mate."

"When you mate?"

"Yes. When I meet another kagu and we do a dance, the kagumambo, and decide we like each other's tail presentation and want to raise a brood of chicks together."

"I see," she said. "And are there lots of kagus in this neighbourhood?"

Pierrot removed his glasses and gave them a little polish. He replaced them on his beak. "Not really, no. I'm the only kagu in Upper Birdland, Lower Birdland and the Passerine Peninsula that I know of." He gazed wistfully into the distance.

"Sooo..." she asked, "why don't you choose to be another bird? Something more common?"

He stared at her in shock. "*Choose?* Are you mad?"

"Well, if you were a parrot, or an owl, for example, I saw lots of both of those at Rookery."

"You used to be such an intelligent little myna. Perhaps when you fell on your head you lost more than just your manners and memory," he said pointedly.

She smiled and parroted back, "perhaps."

"Didn't you study birdology in fledgling school, little myna?"

She shrugged.

"Hmmm. I suppose if you don't remember who you are then you don't remember the facts of flight either." He lifted her new yellow plumage out of the bucket. "I have a box of white feathers on my bureau on the landing. There's also a sewing kit in that drawer. Could you fetch them please? We'll stitch a few white ones into your yellow plumage."

She climbed the small ladder to the house and made her way to the landing. In the second drawer she discovered a collection of red cardboard beaks identical to the one Pierrot was wearing. She smiled and closed the drawer. On top of the bureau was a box with a feather motif carved on the lid. She opened it to verify it contained white feathers, then located the needles and thread and returned, handing them to Pierrot.

"This crest is a bit plumulaceous for a myna," he said, examining the yellow kagu plumage. "Tail's good. But we may need to trim the head feathers..."

"Don't!" she said. "I like them."

He looked at her. "It's not really about liking them little myna, is it?"

"I like them," she repeated.

"Other birds will think you're a myna pretending to be a kagu," he said, as if that were a clinching argument. She giggled gleefully.

"And why is that funny, hmmmm?"

"No reason," she said, giggling some more.

"You know, you were a lot more personable when you were smaller," he wagged his finger at her again.

"Hmmmm. What was the small 'me' like?" she asked, intrigued by his recollection.

"Let's see." He took his glasses off and cleaned them, which he tended to do when he was recollecting things, especially when he knew the answer only too well. "You giggled a lot. You still do that. And you seemed quite proud of the fact that you were nine. And you were very, very clever for your age. As was your friend the loon, though he let you do all the talking for some reason. Also, you were very generous—most mynas are more on the acquisitive side. And you were nice to me, even when I was at the passport desk. That is a rarity in my line of work. Most visiting birds complain about going through customs."

The dye had dried to his satisfaction so he began fastening white feathers in a random spotty pattern.

"Did you miss me... after... when I went away?" she asked.

"Yes... ummm, no, of course not... well a little bit," he stumbled through a range of answers. Finally he said, "yes—very much. I had a wonderful time with you. There aren't all that many tourists in Birdland. Mostly I just sit at my desk and watch the sea."

"I see," she nodded.

"You were the last visitor actually, prior to this visit, so you're the last *two* visitors... can you fetch your winter plumage please little myna?" he asked. "We might as well dye that too, while we're doing this one. It's in the 'Dickenshaw Tailer' bag on the landing."

She disappeared into the house for a few minutes and returned wearing the white plumage with one of his cardboard beaks attached to her nose. Pierrot's eyes went wide. He put his sewing down and stood up, opening his wings and holding them down and forward like a cape while lowering his head, his crest raised and fanned. He began to strut, somewhat comically, legs and elbows akimbo, making small barking sounds.

She waited until his back was turned for a wriggly tail display and leapt back inside the house, returning a few moments later in his nightshirt carrying the kagu plumage.

"Where did she go? Did you see her?" he interrogated Lucy Whatplease in a panic.

"Who?" she asked innocently.

"The kagu! She was just here!"

"Kagu?" she arched a brow. "I thought there were no other kagus in Birdland?"

"The kagu was just here, where you're standing now!"

She shrugged. "Nope, didn't see a kagu. What did she look like?"

"She was around your height, a little on the tall side for a kagu but... she was beautiful, a vision of loveliness! Splendid crown, white downy plumage, tapering red beak, pert tail feathers, and her face... a dream."

"Did you speak to her?"

"No, I was dancing..."

"Dancing? Mmhmmm. Kagumambo was it?"

"That's a bit personal, little myna!"

"I see," she said, smiling.

"We have to find her! You head down to the beach, I'll look in the forest."

"Maybe you were seeing what you wanted to see, Pierrot?"

"Not at all, there was a kagu, I saw her."

"Did she look like me?"

"Oh no. You're a myna. Probably quite pretty for a myna, if somewhat bulky, I really can't tell—myna's all look the same to me. This was a beautiful kagu."

"I'll show you something, wait here." She went inside and collected one of his beaks then returned and told him to watch. She took off the nightgown and slipped on the white plumage, attaching the beak over her nose. His eyes went wide. He pointed his wings down and forward like a cape, lowered his head and fanned his crest. He started to strut and bark.

"Stop it Pierrot!" she said.

He wriggled his tail feathers and bobbed his head, paying no attention. She took off the beak. He paused and looked at her strangely.

"Something's happened to your beak, sweet kagu," he said confused, "is it damaged?"

"It's me, Pierrot. Weren't you watching?"

"What?" he said.

She peeled off the kagu plumage and put the nightshirt back on.

"Naughty myna!" he said. "Well, naughty yes, but what a lucky piece of mischief this time. I was mistaken, you're not a myna at all, you're a kagu! You're a kagu!" he exclaimed excitedly.

She sighed and rolled her eyes. "You're hopeless."

He cogitated a bit. "But that means you weren't ever a myna, you were a juvenile kagu when I met you... a yellow spotted kagu? We need to consult Plumy's *Avis Subterraneus*... never heard of the yellow spotted, extremely rare." He scratched his head. "Rare, yes, that's why we thought you were a myna!"

"I'm never putting the plumage back on if you're going to do that silly dance," she said.

He looked at her oddly. "But," he said, "it's what I do?"

"It's not what I do," she said. "Let's try something..." She took off the nightshirt and put on the yellow plumage. His eyes went wide and she quickly took it off. She sighed again.

"What's wrong?" he asked.

"It's not that I don't like you, Pierrot," she said. "I like you very much. You're kind and sweet, but..." she looked at him earnestly, "I don't know who I am yet and I don't want to mate with you and raise chicks in the family nest if I don't know where I come from or how I got here."

"Ah," said Pierrot. "Quite so. But I can help you there. Clean up the mystery in a jiffy."

He pulled her passport out of his wing pocket and handed it to her. "This is you," he said. "Ignore the bit that says myna, we were mistaken about that."

"Lucy is a nice name."

"Lucy Whatplease! Yes, that's your name, little myn... little kagu," he corrected.

"It says I'm nine years old, Pierrot." She frowned.

"Ha," he waved a wing dismissively, "that was two years ago."

"I don't know how old I am, Pierrot, but I'm not eleven."

"Yes," he said, scratching his chin. "Bit mysterious. We should consult Professor Tweet, he's an expert on avian ageing."

"Somehow, I don't think this Lucy is me."

"I guarantee it's you, little kagu."

"Guarantee? How?"

"Well it has to be you, doesn't it. Simple logic. Look at the likeness."

She looked at the hand drawn flower and sighed again. "I can tell that you want it to be me, but I don't see any logic—simple or otherwise—Pierrot."

"Well, you probably don't remember how logic works without your memory."

"How do you explain that I'm an adult instead of eleven years old?"

"I can't, of course... but that only means I can't, I'm sure Professor Tweet will have an explanation."

She shook her head.

He continued, "If a tree floated past us upside-down right now, and we both saw it but had no explanation, would that mean there was no tree, or that we have no explanation?"

"Hmmm," she said, unconvinced. "You're appealing to *Pupril's Law of Limited Dichotomies*. Could there not also be a situation where we are floating upside down and the tree is static and upright?"

"Ah!" countered Pierrot, "your new clause is over-reliant on *Gagphager's Principle of the Imaginary Real*."

"But," she said, "is not the original conjecture, namely the presence of an inverted soaring topiary, appealing to Gagphager's first clause of that very principle? Let's try a different conjecture. If we traded leaves, let's say I give you a set price of 22 yellow ones and you give me 22 red ones..."

"Yes!" he said, clapping, "that would be an *excellent* trade."

"But," she said, "you pay the full 22 leaf levy in a single instalment and I counter with two instalments, the first of nine leaves and the second of two leaves. Would you feel cheated by that transaction?"

"That would depend, I suppose, on your authority in the field of botany."

"How so?" she inquired.

"An expert valuation on the leaves might accord higher value to yellow pigmentation. *Thurbinger's Law of Equilibrious Harmony* ultimately overrides any perceived numerical inequalities, replacing them with equal and opposing values in the realm of the actual."

"The fallacy in this equation has the dimensions of a dance floor where tautologies caper and twirl beyond the reach of criticism."

Pierrot made a dismissive hand gesture. "Straw Bird and *Ad Avianum* arguments generate too little value to bother refuting."

"So, what—out of idle curiosity—did you pay the Dickenshaws

for this plumage?"

"Two brand new passports, latest stamps, they were very pleased."

"Passports? Are they going somewhere?"

"Oh no, parrots aren't a migratory species. Never left Rookery in their lives to the best of my knowledge."

"Then why do they need passports?"

"Everyone needs a passport."

"Your world is filled with interactions that make little sense Pierrot."

"*Our world* little kagu. And the interactions make perfect sense. We just don't always know what that perfect sense is. That's how the world works. It does what it does even when we don't know why it's doing what it's doing." He smiled, pleased with his own excellent grasp of the way things are. "You'll understand all this when your memory and powers of deduction return, little kagu."

"I don't think I'm a kagu, Pierrot."

"I know you are. Very obvious now. Though you should put your plumage on. You're quite beautiful in your plumage… devastating in fact, bird-walk material."

She shrugged her shoulders.

"Please," he said.

"Will you promise not to dance and bark?"

He digested her request. "Yes," he responded.

She put on the yellow spotted plumage.

"And the beak," he asked hopefully.

She shook her head.

"You're gorgeous even with a broken beak," he said admiringly, "but simply stunning with your full beak."

She ignored his plea and returned the cardboard beak to his bureau. "You may continue to call me Lucy until we discover my real name" she advised him.

3 | Academy

"Yes, it's her all right. Confirmed. Absolutely no question."

"A yellow spotted kagu who used to be a myna?" queried Professor Tweet, skeptically. "There's no mention of yellow spotted kagu in *Avis Subterraneus*. No mention in Pugwiler's *Advanced Guide to Exotic Birds* either, although Trinket's *Bird Encyclopedia* does suggest an archaic—now extinct—species of kagu that may have been spotted, with or without rings around its neck."

"There you go then," said Pierrot emphatically. "Not extinct after all. Newly rediscovered."

"Could be a leucistic variant," suggested Saddleback, shrugging.

"But a juvenile stage resembling a myna is still problematic, Saddleback," said Brightfeather.

"Or not!" said Professor Tweet, overriding his junior colleagues with a portentous tone. "The life cycle of any long extinct species is open to conjecture… a real feather in our crests if we can fill in some of the blanks. We'll need to study her, of course. She could well be the *find of our generation!*"

"Study her?" said Pierrot with a concerned expression. "Ummm, what exactly does that entail?"

"Well," said Brightfeather without hesitation, "we'll need to include her skeleton in the collection, she'll be the Type Specimen for her species…. after a proper dissection of course. No one's ever seen an archaic syrinx—that will reveal fascinating insights under the scalpel!"

Pierrot squawked loudly and flapped his wings in a panic.

"When she dies," added Tweet, soothingly. "When she dies."

"Oh?" said Brightfeather, peevishly, "but she's so young—what if she outlives all of us? You want a junior faculty upstart to take all the glory for documenting this discovery? That precocious fellow Keel for example?"

Tweet hastily signalled to Brightfeather to drop the subject in the presence of Pierrot who was clearly distressed.

Saddleback caught on quickly and chuckled nervously. "Brightfeather, really—poor Pierrot can't be expected to share your perverse sense of humour now, can he?"

Brightfeather furrowed his brow at Saddleback, then the coin dropped and he made an oops gesture to his colleagues. "Ha ha," he said unconvincingly, "academic humour," he turned to Pierrot. "We do enjoy our little jokes in the faculty."

"Ahem," said Saddleback, looking askance at Tweet. "If I recall correctly, this yellow spotted has an honorary degree in ornithology from this very university. Technically she's alumni, privileges, et al." He raised a brow.

"We might need to revisit the rulebook," Tweet replied in a whisper that was less discrete than he imagined.

Pierrot, finally able to speak coherently, spoke forcefully. "NO ONE," he said, "touches a feather on her yellow spotted crest."

"Kagu," whispered Brightfeather, with a wink to his colleagues, "are *very* territorial—mate for life you know."

"We are not your students, Professor Brightfeather," retorted Tweet with a hint of disdain.

"Teaching your grandmother to lay eggs," added Saddleback, who sided with the pompous Tweet against the pompous Brightfeather whenever possible.

❄ ❄ ❄

Pierrot was held up by some customs business arising unexpectedly at the university—a pair of shady looking exchange students, crows from Lower Birdland, required urgent study visas. On completion of his duties he hurried home and met Lucy on the steps of his house talking to a pair of officious looking men in magpie plumage.

"These two are looking for a yellow spotted kagu, Pierrot. I explained to them that no such species exists to the best of my knowledge," she giggled. "They seem keen to search your house."

"Passports please," said Pierrot to the magpies.

"What?" said one.

"This is a restricted customs area! Your passports—quickly now."

"We're on official business," said one, showing his Rookery Magpie badge. "We have reason to believe the occupant of this house is harbouring a fugiti…"

"I'm not interested in your badge," said Pierrot, sternly. "And I won't ask again. I want to see your passports *and* a permit that allows you to be in this highly restricted Kagu area… *well!!*"

They looked at one another. One said menacingly, "You better be more cooperative when we come back."

"And you'd better have all your paperwork in order when you do," responded Pierrot.

Lucy was surprised to see Pierrot so assertive, she was quietly impressed and she told him so as soon as the magpies were out of earshot.

"We have no time, young kagu," he said. "We have to leave. Your playfulness saved your skin, but they'll be back and we won't be so lucky next time."

She looked at him confused.

"I'm sorry, I'll explain the situation once we're safely away. This is my fault, I made a miscalculation. Collect your white plumage, that will be a handy disguise, and your yellow spotted of course. Put it on now"

The urgency in his voice convinced Lucy that he was serious so she followed his instructions. Pierrot filled a satchel with seedbread and added some personal effects and they set off in the opposite direction to the magpies, towards the Passerine Peninsula.

4 | Flight

An orangutan mechanic in yellow overalls with a passing resemblance to a canary greeted them. "Your business?"

"We are flight instructors. Well, I'm a qualified flight instructor, this is my student, Ms Whatplease. She's here for a flying lesson." Pierrot flashed his golden wings.

"Kagu's are flightless, no?" the mechanic said, bemused.

"Precisely. That makes her the perfect bird to get flight lessons!"

He scratched his orange chin. "Which craft will you be taking?" he asked.

"Your fastest," replied Pierrot. "This one's a daredevil," he indicated towards Lucy. *"Young kagus,"* he added in a 'you-know-what-they're-like' tone with a wink.

The mechanic led them to a tandem bicycle with broad feathery wings and a stiff rudder. It had solid ring fastenings at the front and back. "I'll find you some balloons," he said.

He wheeled a sand trolley with a dozen straining blue balloons to the aircraft and attached them one by one to the rings. It pulled skyward against its sandbag restraints.

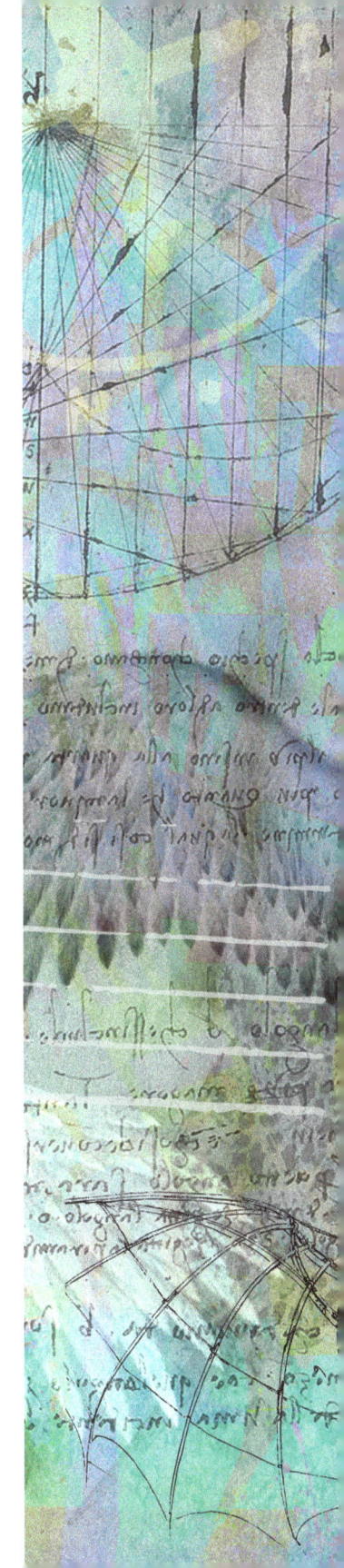

"Haven't actually flown this model, eh what," said Pierrot, trying to sound like a seasoned pilot.

"Pedals flap the wings," sighed the mechanic, "rear seat has the rudder, front seat the flaps, like all the others. Are you sure you're an instructor?"

"Would you like to see my gold wing badge again?" asked Pierrot, with more than a hint of superiority.

"Pedals flap the wings, rear seat has the rudder, front seat the flaps," Pierrot said to Lucy in his most instructor-like voice. "That will do nicely, my good fellow," Pierrot said to the mechanic, "I'll take it from here."

"Right you are, *Mr Instructor*," said the mechanic, with a liberal dose of sarcasm. Lucy giggled and winked at him.

They wheeled the tandem out to the airstrip, sandbags dragging and bumping along the tarmac. Pierrot took the rudder seat and Lucy climbed in the front saddle. Pierrot untied the sandbags and they were instantly aloft. They began pedalling to get the wings flapping lazily, which added almost nothing to their speed, the craft mostly drifting on the breeze.

Lucy looked down and saw a commotion. Two magpies were pointing at them and arguing with the mechanic. They were too far away to hear what was being said, but this was the airfield's fastest craft after all, and they had a significant lead. After a while they drifted over the tree line, across a series of reefs and out to sea.

❄ ❄ ❄

At sunrise they were drifting west with the rising sun at their backs. Both had long stopped pedalling—a frisky breeze doing the work—and Pierrot was snoring loudly. The blue-black ocean slid beneath their wheels. Lucy looked over her shoulder and caught a sun-glint in the distance. She fixed her gaze on that point and saw there was another craft. She tapped Pierrot's knee. He woke up with a snort.

"We're being followed," she said, in an urgent whisper.

"What?" he said, looking over his shoulder and adjusting his spectacles. "Oh no, the magpies."

They pedalled vigorously and their pursuers started to recede.

4 | Flight

After 30 minutes the horizon before them became jagged and after another 40 minutes they were flying over land.

It was a strange landscape: broken trees, blackened holes and muddy ditches stained with red patches. One hillside village they flew over was reduced to rubble and Lucy thought she could make out furtive figures darting between the broken piles of stone and brick. A booming sound, like muffled thunder, punctuated the eerie silence and an odd unpleasant smell hung in the air.

Weary from pedalling, a quick glance astern confirmed that the magpies were gaining on them again.

Pierrot's knees were clicking loudly and he was grunting with each ungainly push on the pedals—he was clearly uncomfortable. They slowed to a drift at Lucy's insistence and twenty minutes later the magpies were alongside them, within touching distance.

"Pull over," shouted one through an unnecessary cardboard megaphone. "You're under arrest."

"Passports please," Pierrot shouted back, perversely.

Lucy reached behind her and pulled on Pierrot's beak. The elastic snapped. She jabbed at the magpies' balloons. One exploded, then another. Their craft began a slow spiralling descent, its occupants squawking and flapping and hurling threats as they drifted toward the ground.

"Oops, I'm sorry, I lost your beak," she motioned to Pierrot who was still in beak-loss shock. "Magpie knocked it from my grip," she said.

Pierrot held a hand over his nose and looked at her wide-eyed. He struggled to say anything for a while, then finally mumbled, "I suppose it's fitting that we're both beakless… you saved us, little myna… little kagu… Lucy."

"For now," she pointed down. "They'll likely follow us on the ground—they might be faster than us."

The pair pedalled lazily as the sun rose in the sky.

"I think you're a handsome kagu, even without your beak," she said eventually, pondering his discomfort.

He smiled, and—after thinking for a while—said "You're very unusual for a kagu, Lucy Whatplease."

"Am I?" she said, indifferent to the accusation. "So, what did those magpies want with us Pierrot?"

"Ah, yes. That."

She waited for him to explain.

"I let some professors—Tweet, Brightfeather and Saddleback—know that you're a kagu. Apparently, it turns out, you're a no longer extinct yellow spotted species—they got rather excited. They want to study you."

"Study me?"

"Study you... in a *display your skeleton at the academy* sort of way."

"Oh. I see."

"I had no idea Lucy. I'm sorry. Those magpies are not pursuing us to extend a dinner invitation."

"Clearly not." She thought about their dilemma for a while then asked, "are all the birds in Birdland like you Pierrot?"

"Like me? Oh goodness no. I'm the only kagu in Birdland, aside from you of course."

"No, I mean, you thought I was a myna when I was dressed as one. Then you thought I was a kagu when I wore kagu plumage. If I wear albatross feathers with a curved beak, you'll think I'm an albatross. Are all birdlanders like that?"

"What a ridiculous observation Lucy—you're a kagu. You'd just be pretending to be an albatross and no one sensible would do that or be fooled by that."

"The magpies didn't know I was a kagu when I was wearing your nightshirt... if we both wear nightshirts, maybe they won't see us. They'll walk past looking for kagus."

He scratched his chin. "That doesn't sound right to me, it's obvious that we're both kagus," said Pierrot.

"Obvious how?"

"Well the kagu crest is very distinctive, and the chest and tail display too, and the dapper ruffled whitish plumage set against a shiny red beak..."

"Will you just trust me and do something if I ask you to, Pierrot?" she inquired earnestly.

He thought about the request. "Well," he said, "you're quite a long way in credit on the Thurbinger Scale... so yes, just ask."

"Take off your plumage. Two nightshirts are in my satchel. Wear one of those."

"My plumage?" he said, slightly shocked. She said nothing more. He slipped out of his upper plumage, stowing it in his satchel, and pulled on the knee-length night shirt. The pair pedalled in silence.

By midday storm clouds were gathering on the horizon. Lucy pulled on a lever under her seat to tilt the wing flaps and the craft descended gently, finally landing with a few bounces across vehicular ruts in a small country lane.

The lane had a hedge on one side and a dry stone wall on the other. Wildflowers spilled through the hedge and tumbled over a ditch that bordered a grassy paddock. It was a manicured landscape, nothing like the blackened, smoking fields they'd flown over earlier. They wheeled their craft through a gap in the hedge and used its dangling guy-ropes to secure it to an oak tree.

Lucy changed into a nightdress. Pierrot removed the lower parts of his plumage, adding them to his satchel. He had a sense of being terribly vulnerable in just his nestwear away from his nest, so he chirped quietly to quell his anxieties. Having secured the bag to their craft and placed a marker on the hedge, they set off on foot in a westerly direction, hoping to find shelter ahead of the rain clouds that were bearing down on them.

A white van with a smiling cow painted on its side appeared, rattling down the lane, heading in their direction. It pulled up when it reached them and the driver—a corpulent, rosy-cheeked man in white overalls and a grey cheese cutter—leaned out the window. "Storm's caught you out," he said, squinting at the heavy skies ahead, "I can give you a lift to town if you don't mind a circus… there's a fresh slaughtered pig, lamb sausages and a pair of lunatics in the back," he said to Pierrot with a grin. "Your girlfriend can ride up front with me."

"I'll be ok in the back," said Lucy, smiling broadly. "Thank you for your kindness."

"Suit yourself."

They opened the back door. Seated on a low wooden bench along one side, surrounded by glistening offal, were the magpies. Pierrot froze but Lucy climbed straight in and motioned for him to follow. Both the magpies cocked their heads at the new arrivals with an air of mild confusion.

"Are you two from around here?" one asked suspiciously.

"Yes," said Lucy. "Out for a stroll. I've not seen you in these parts though. Where are you two from?"

"Official business," said one of them.

"Classified," said the other.

"Tracking a fugitive," said the first, ignoring his companion. "Kagu, yellow spotted. Tall bird with a fancy crest. Red beak. Unusual plumage."

"Show off species—kagus are worse than peacocks," chimed the other. "You seen her? She's travelling with another kagu. Blue-white. Tall. Spectacles. Shifty look. Argumentative."

"Nasty piece of work," added the other. "Both of them I imagine."

"I warned you it was a circus back there," said the driver, chuckling through the grill.

"We've not seen any birds answering that description," said Lucy to the magpies, the way a nurse might speak to a delirious patient, "but if we do, we'll let you know." She winked at Pierrot who's expression of panic was beginning to fade.

"Out for a stroll in your night clothes?" asked the driver, putting his van into gear.

"My friend is a sleep walker," she improvised, "and so am I."

The driver nodded slowly.

"You're a butcher?" She changed the subject.

"That I am, Gristle the butcher. Finest viands, delicacies and smoked cuts in the district."

Light rain speckled the van windows as they bumped down the lane.

"But being a local, you'd know that already," he suggested.

"Your reputation for quality meats is common knowledge, Mr Gristle," Lucy replied. "Though my companion and I are vegetarian and unworldly in such matters."

The rain gained momentum, quickly becoming heavy and insistent, a dull hammering racket inside the van punctuated by the rhythmic thump of wiper blades. The lane wound up a hillside strewn with rocks and flint-grass. It passed through a wall arch into Upper Swell, a quaint hamlet where stone architecture overhung cobbled streets with a variety of shops and stalls lining the avenue leading to the town square. Gristle stopped outside the Poacher's

Arms, a cosy looking tavern.

"You'll want to wait out the storm in there," said Gristle. "And being in your night clothes I don't suppose you're carrying cash… tell that rogue Harbinger, the innkeeper, to put your expenses on my tab. You can settle the account next time you come to town."

"That's very generous indeed," said Pierrot, finding his voice.

"Thank you very much Mr Gristle," said Lucy.

"You two," he addressed the magpies, "I'll take you to someone who can help you on your 'secret mission'," he winked at Lucy.

"Very good," said one.

"Chop chop," said the other. "Time's of the essence."

5 | Shelter

The inn featured a series of alcoves that circled an open hearth where a fire was freshly lit to combat the unseasonal weather. The pair selected a seat near the fire.

Gristle had not resembled a bird of any sort and neither did any of the inn's patrons. Pierrot was confused.

"Maybe people aren't birds in these lands," Lucy offered in response.

Pierrot was unsatisfied with her speculation. He turned to a short, badger-like man at the next table. "Excuse me. If you don't mind me asking, what species are you?"

The man looked at him quizzically. He had short cropped hair, beady eyes and a prominent nose that hung over his mouth and chin. His burly physique and leather apron suggested a tradesman of some sort. "Species? Is this a clever insult?"

"I wondered on account of your lack of a beak or tail?" persisted Pierrot.

The badger man growled and started to rise to his feet. Lucy quickly got up and stepped forward. "I'm terribly sorry," she said. "My friend hasn't been himself since he lost his own beak and plumage."

The man looked at her with a furrowed brow, then sighed and sat down.

"It's like that then, you both escaped from the loony bin… explains the nightgowns."

Pierrot began to protest but Lucy turned him around and sat him down, then plumped into her own seat. "Careful Pierrot," she whispered. "We have to be a little bit circumspect about what we say to whom, at least until we have our bearings. These people aren't Birdlanders. We don't know what constitutes bad manners here."

He nodded.

The innkeeper paused at their table. "A fine stormy afternoon to come to town in your nightdresses," he said, raising an eyebrow. "I hope you're not planning on spending the day drying yourself by my fire. That warmth's for my paying patrons."

"Good day, Mr Harbinger," Lucy replied with a broad smile. "Our mutual friend Mr Gristle suggested we avail ourselves of your hospitality with a tab against his name."

"Gristle?" he said, bemused. "That old crook! All right then, I'll get Rosie to bring you a menu. As Master Gristle is paying we'll rouse our top chef from his siesta and find you something expensive to drink from the cellar. Next time he sends us one of his padded accounts for offal and third grade meat, we'll send an even more expensive one back to make him rethink his prices."

"That won't be necessary," said Lucy. "A simple dish of lentils and bread will suffice, and two mugs of water. We're both modest in our appetites."

Harbinger pursed his lips. "That barely comes to 3 talons—surely you'd like something more elaborate?"

"No really, we're fine with lentils," said Lucy. Pierrot nodded.

Harbinger shrugged and made his way back to the bar. A short time later their food and water was served. The barmaid, a cheerful young woman with pigtails and freckles, expressed curiosity about their attire.

"We had to leave home in a hurry," Lucy explained.

"Ah," she nodded. "The war. Only a matter of time before it spreads to West Falde. You've come from the east then. Are you from one of the coastal fishing villages?"

"We're from Birdland," said Pierrot. "We crossed the ocean and we didn't see any villages near the coast. Just smoke and ruins."

The barmaid looked alarmed by his description of East Falde.

"Are you Rosie?" asked Lucy.

Rosie nodded.

"I'm Lucy and this is Pierrot."

She smiled. "I've not heard of Birdland, is it a long way from Falde?"

"Only a day or so by modern aircraft," answered Pierrot. "Perhaps two days as the crow flies."

"And… you have no belongings or money, just the clothes you're wearing?" inquired Rosie.

"I have a few Birdland dollars," said Pierrot. "Had," he corrected himself, remembering that he kept his wallet in the wing pocket of his plumage.

"What is this war about, Rosie?" asked Lucy.

"It's a civil war," she explained. "The People's Party, who were the old tyrants in government, lost the last election. They complained that the election was rigged by the Worker's Party, who won, so they demanded a re-election, which was definitely rigged—the People's Party won 100% of the votes in that one. Half of the Falde Army is with the People's Party, but some generals broke away and formed the Worker's Militia. They've been fighting each other in East Falde."

"So the People's Party are the bad ones?" suggested Pierrot, struggling to comprehend the picture she'd drawn.

"Oh no!" Rosie replied, "the Worker's Party are a pack of old tyrants too. Each party's main focus is to make a small group of very rich people very very rich. It's just that within that small group are two smaller groups that want to be richer than each other. That's really what the war is about."

"So…." asked Pierrot, "the war is rich people fighting each other?"

Rosie giggled. "You really are from a distant land, aren't you? No, only folks like you and me are risking their lives on the front line. The rich have soirees and go falconing together and place wagers on various battles. The generals of both armies meet for brandy after a day's fighting. They're all friends regardless of the side they're on."

"That's madness," said Pierrot. "Why do people allow it?"

"It's just the way things are," shrugged Rosie. "Rich folk control the army and the police who protect their assets and uphold the status quo. They do what they like. What can we do? People in West Falde just get on with life and ignore what goes on in the East and hope it doesn't spread. Though, that said, we've got recruitment booths for both factions across the square."

Rosie departed to serve some new arrivals at the bar. Pierrot scratched his chin. "They're all mad!" he whispered to Lucy. "That's the oddest thing I've ever heard."

"Maybe," said Lucy after a few moments of contemplation, "everyone's a bit crazy, here, and in Birdland… you and me too, we all just do different versions of crazy."

"Why on earth would you think that, little kagu? Birdlanders don't have wars! No one in Birdland would risk lives just because someone ordered them to, especially when the orders make no sense."

"Not even a magpie?"

"Hmmm," said Pierrot.

"Perhaps… what makes sense is what you think makes sense, Pierrot," she continued. "I have no memory of being a myna or a kagu, so being a bird doesn't make a lot of sense to me. Maybe I'll recover all my memories and then things that seem strange will seem less strange. Or maybe I won't remember who I am and everything will always be a little bit nonsensical."

She furrowed her brow. "And speaking of magpies, I'm worried about our pair. Mr Gristle might not have been as helpful to them as he was to us."

"You should be relieved if he's been unhelpful, young kagu. The less helpful the better with those two."

For the rest of the afternoon the rain fell in surges between heavy and very heavy. Pierrot and Lucy sought modest lodgings from the innkeeper for the night. The cheapest he could supply—for the addition of three talons to Gristle's account—was in the loft above the stable with straw for bedding. Pierrot was particularly happy with that arrangement, fashioning two comfortable nests with practised ease.

6 | Asylum

The sun rose in a cloudless sky and was greeted by a dawn chorus of tui, pheasant, warbler, kaka, robin, tawny owl, finch and wren, all singing, warbling, tweeting, rawking, cooing and hooting.

"Ha—I knew it!" announced Pierrot gleefully. "Birds! Lots of birds. They *are* normal here!"

He pushed open the loft shutters and was greeted with the sight of fantails chasing each other playfully between the bowers of a row of apple trees that lined the verge. A fat wood pigeon sat on a thin branch, looking back at him with a bobbing head. A group of three tuis were doing unfeasible acrobatics in the sky directly above the trees while a pheasant shuffled around their roots.

"But I can't see them?" he frowned, confused.

Lucy looked out the window and smiled. "Aren't they gorgeous, Pierrot?" she said.

She pulled a comb from a carry bag that held their meagre possessions and set about unknotting her hair, which had acquired quite a lot of straw from the bedding.

He shook his head. The smaller version of Lucy had been a lot easier to understand. Pierrot wondered how much of that was due to her head knock and how much was from her not being nine anymore. Or perhaps from losing the steadying influence of her loon companion. On balance, he thought nine was probably the most excellent age for a kagu, judging from his own experiences with nine-year-old kagus, and although this adventure was a little less enchanting than the previous two, she always seemed to do the exact right thing, which was something special.

His reverie was broken by a sound below. Rosie climbed the ladder into the loft with a basket containing a loaf of rye bread, a creamy cheese, some currants, grapes, tomatoes, freshly churned butter and a bag of oats. "On the house," she said, placing them beside the trapdoor. "Our rooms come with breakfast and you two could probably use a lunch as well. Don't mention it to old Harbinger though. He'll likely charge Master Gristle a king's ransom just out of spite."

"Ooo," squealed Lucy, delighted. Pierrot bowed deeply and solemnly, causing Lucy and Rosie both to giggle.

"There's an out-house around the back with hot water for washing if you haven't found it already," she said.

"If I may ask a question," Pierrot motioned toward the window, "where are the birds? I hear them but don't see any?"

Rosie looked out through the shutters. "Perhaps your spectacles could do with a clean?" she offered. "I count… 7, 8, 9, 10…. 11." She motioned with her index finger as she counted them off.

Lucy chimed in, "the birds might be a bit bigger in Birdland. Is Mr Gristle's shop nearby? I'd really like to thank him for his generosity."

"Directly across the square," Rosie said. "Give him my regards and tell him his tab has been cleared—a late arrival at the tavern looking for lodgings thought you two had the last proper room and overpaid to move you out to the stables—I forgot to mention to him you were already in the stables," she winked. "There were a few talons over so I put them in the basket with your breakfast. And have safe travels," she added. "I'd keep moving west if I were you."

She disappeared back down the ladder with a smile and a wave.

Pierrot was still mulling over the invisible birds. "Has everyone but me had a knock to the head," he asked, not expecting a reply and not getting one.

Gristle the butcher was putting out a sandwich board of specials when he was hailed by Lucy and Pierrot from across the square. They met outside his shop.

"Good day, Master Gristle," said Pierrot, as formally as possible.

"Hiya!" said Lucy with a beaming smile.

"And good day to you two," he replied, doffing his cap. "I trust Harbinger put you up in his most expensive rooms and stuffed you with his finest victuals?" he said with a chuckle.

"Not at all," replied Lucy. "Our needs are modest and your tab was wiped clean by another traveller. People are terribly generous in Upper Swell."

Gristle shook his head with amusement.

"Your generosity, however, sets a benchmark few can hope to match. Thank you very much for providing us with your line of credit." She curtsied.

"What a charming creature you have for a companion," he said to Pierrot. He turned back to Lucy. "I was expecting Harbinger to march into my store demanding a month's free supplies. Naturally I barter him up to a discount which is just above what I charge my other customers. It's a game we play."

Pierrot nodded in a worldly fashion and said "just so", adding an urbane hand gesture as he thought that might impress the butcher, though he struggled to see why Harbinger and Gristle would engage in such a silly contest in the first place.

"Out of interest," asked Lucy, "what happened to those two fellows who were in your van yesterday?"

"I took them to the hospital on yonder hill," he pointed, "and introduced them to Doctor Flaystik. And that's where I left them. They'll get the care they need up there."

"Care?" asked Pierrot, eyebrows knitted. "Was there something wrong with them? Aside from being magpies and all that implies, of course."

"I'm no psychoanalyst… just a butcher, me. You should direct your questions to the doctor. But I'd say the magpie outfits were a decent clue there was no proper meat in that pair of sandwiches," he concluded.

"What sort of hospital might that be?" asked Lucy with a slightly perplexed look.

"Folk call it the loony bin in these parts," said Gristle, tapping his nose. "If you do go up there, I'd suggest you find some day clothes. You don't want them to find you too interesting, if you get my drift."

Lucy nodded and thanked Gristle again for his kindness and promised that if she ever gave up vegetarianism she would be his best customer. They wished him farewell and left him to his business.

Crossing the square they were halted by a man in a forest green uniform. It was buttoned down the front and had bushy silver epaulettes and a jaunty cap with a star at its centre.

"Ah, two new recruits, excellent!" he said.

"Sorry, what?" asked Pierrot.

"What... please?" said Lucy, taken by surprise.

"The People's Party of Falde is the party of the people," he said, earnestly.

Pierrot shook his head. "No thank you."

"We can have you in uniform in a day and fighting at the front in two, and your pretty lady friend will be a fully qualified nurse patching up the boys at the front in just four." He beamed a smile that was sincere, warm and serious.

"No, thank you," repeated Pierrot.

"Oh," he said, "you want to join the navy. Wise choice. See the world as a boy, come back a man."

"I said no thank you, please move out of the way."

The recruitment officer for the Royal Falde Expeditionary Forces turned to Lucy. "What a pretty one you are, Miss. Think of those poor boys with arms and legs missing, purblind with shell-shock and cut in half by landmines. They'll see you—with eyes that have looked into the black heart of war—as an angel, a beacon of hope, a reason to get themselves back to the front, to save their wives and sisters from those sadistic devils of the Worker's Militia. Think of the comfort and inspiration you can give them."

"She's not interested," said Pierrot forcefully.

"Or a comfort girl—who would begrudge our brave boys at the front a little pleasure?"

"Passport please!" said Pierrot in his most official voice.

"What?" said the recruitment officer, looking confused.

"I need to see your passport... NOW!"

The recruitment officer took a step back. "Woah," he said. He looked left and right. "Has this town fallen to the Militia? Oh hell!"

He pointed over Pierrot's shoulder and shouted "LOOK!"

Pierrot and Lucy both turned and saw nothing. They turned back to see the recruitment officer for the Royal Falde Expeditionary Forces running at full tilt down the road heading east out of town.

A hand clapped on Pierrot's shoulder accompanied by a hearty laugh. "Out-*bloody*-standing!" said a man in a forest green uniform with gold epaulettes and three stars on the cap who was the recruitment officer for the Worker's Militia. "Black ops for you, ranking officer in three months. Undercover. Best raw recruitment material I've seen. Don't worry, we'll look after your girlfriend. We need the pretty ones for honeytraps, they make excellent spies." He winked at Lucy.

"May I see your passport?" growled Pierrot.

"What?" said the recruitment officer for the Worker's Militia.

Lucy put a finger up to her ear and spoke to no one, "roger that, target acquired. Repeat, target acquired. Confirm. Green, three stars, at 9 o'clock, over."

The recruitment officer for the Worker's Militia ducked down and ran a mad zigzag across the square, disappearing down the eastern road at a sprint.

Pierrot looked at Lucy with admiration. "I don't know what any of that means, what you just said, but you scared the daylights out of him."

"I don't know what it means either," she said. "I'm getting little flashes of memory but nothing to tie the fragments together or make sense of them."

"There's a lot more to you than meets the eye, young kagu," he said, shaking his head.

❊ ❊ ❊

"Where are they now?" asked Lucy Whatplease.

"I handed them over, restrained, of course, to the military police."

Dr Flaystik was a sinuous man who seemed to slide around inside his clothes. His face was narrow with a prominent nose that bisected high cheekbones and close-set, half-closed eyes.

"They presented with classical paranoid delusion, but of course paranoia isn't infectious. There were two of them exhibiting identical symptoms. The chances of that occurring randomly are probably less than one in twenty—maybe twenty five—thousand. And that makes it some sort of ruse, you see. We have instructions from the highest levels, suspicious characters have to be handed over to the PB for interrogation. There are spies trying to infiltrate West Falde, you know." He smiled thinly at Lucy, then at Pierrot. "So what exactly is your interest in them?"

"PB?" asked Lucy.

"Patriot Bureau."

"What were their symptoms?"

"They insisted they were birds, magpies. Said they were chasing a pair of fugitive birds! You can't make that stuff up, well maybe you can. PB will find out one way or another."

"I'm sorry," said Pierrot, "being a bird is a symptom of what?"

"An unhinged mind, obviously" said Flaystik. "You were going to explain your interest in them?"

"We were offered a ride in Mr Gristle's van after he picked them up," Lucy cut in before Pierrot could continue. "We thought they were actors or comedians. We were shocked to hear that they'd been hospitalised so we came to visit them and say hello as we thought they might not have family in Upper Swell."

"I see," said Flaystik, visibly relaxing. "Why the nightshirts, if you don't mind me asking?"

"We've travelled from the east," said Lucy. "War has the entire coast by the throat, we had to leave quickly, under cover of darkness."

"Ah yes, war is the necessary evil, let's hope it doesn't spread to our quiet corner."

"Thank you for your time, Dr Flaystik," said Lucy. "If they're spies they'll be deservedly locked away and I'm sure PB will release them if they're not." She smiled disarmingly and Flaystik smiled back.

"Charming creature, your companion. I observe you're a lucky man," he said to Pierrot.

"Lucy is the kindest person I know," said Pierrot, cleaning his spectacles on his shirt. "And I'm beginning to think the smartest."

❉ ❉ ❉

"I hear you have some magpies in the lock up," Lucy winked

conspiratorially at the Military Policeman standing in front of the main doors of the Patriot Bureau, a large, windowless stone and brick building two streets from the Upper Swell main square. She giggled flirtatiously.

"Had," said the guard, grinning back. "Sent them back to the loony bin, mad as snakes they are."

"Too crazy to be spies, huh?"

"Any sane person would tell what they know under Bureau interrogation," he said, leaving little to imagine as to what 'interrogation' meant. "But they just twittered about being official magpies."

"Obviously crazy."

"I like the fashion statement," he eyed her up and down. "I finish my shift at six—I'll be at the Poacher's Arms."

She winked at him again and continued down the street where Pierrot was waiting around the corner.

"They tortured the magpies and sent them back to the hospital," said Lucy, visibly upset.

Pierrot grimaced.

"We have to rescue them, Pierrot."

"Rescue them!" he stepped back alarmed.

"You heard what Flaystik said—saying you're a bird is a symptom of an unhinged mind! Tell me, do you have an unhinged mind?"

Pierrot looked at her with raised brows.

"No of course you don't. What does it mean to be mad in a mad world anyway? We have to rescue them."

"But Lucy, the magpies want to take you back to the University of Rookery to be studied."

"The magpies didn't recognise either of us without feathers, Pierrot. They see the world through a lens that only reveals the reality they know. Anyway, maybe their priorities are changing."

"Why do these magpies matter to you?"

"They're people. Their misguided mission is to escort us back to Birdland. Maybe they should succeed? This place is not safe for you, Pierrot. What's happening to them right now, it could happen to you too."

"What do you mean?" he looked at her sideways, a curiously bird-like gesture.

"If you were still wearing your plumage you'd be in the hospital on the hill. It's only a matter of time before you reveal who you are. You're a bird, Pierrot, a kagu. Hiding your identity in this place is only a temporary solution."

"And… I take it you think you're *not* a kagu?"

"I don't know who I am. I could be a kagu, or a myna, but those are memories I can't access. I think we have to rescue the magpies for our own sakes. They're only here because we are."

❊ ❊ ❊

It was a soft night. They lay on their backs in an open field, illuminated by a scattering of stars.

"What's that one called?" she pointed at the brightest light in the ink black sky.

"The Dog Star."

Lucy smiled. "I love dogs."

"Never met one," Pierrot replied, "what are they like?"

"Adorable… playful… focused… transparent in all their emotions and desires. They create a universe around themselves according to how they perceive things."

"Mhm?"

"They lick you because they think you're their puppy and you need a jolly good cleaning—they're very responsible parents… but they also want you to stroke them because you're their mother and your hand is your tongue."

Pierrot tried to digest that.

"And they love fetching balls and sticks," said Lucy.

"Ha! I knew a loon like that. He was your companion."

"Tell me about him."

"Not sure where to start… he was very partial to retrieving balls. But the way he did it made other birds happy. He was very clever."

"Did he have four legs?"

"Oh yes, four legs are a feature of the rare nocturnal loon."

"And I'm guessing he barked?"

"Limited vocabulary, accident at birth."

Lucy smiled at the night sky. "I think you'd probably like dogs, if you ever get to meet any."

※ ※ ※

"Mr Glopp is it? The barmaid said you're in charge of the nurses at the hospital." She nodded towards the bar where Rosie waved back. "I'm Lucy, would you mind if I join you?"

Glopp indicated for her to sit at his table with a cultured flourish. "A bit early for a nightdress," he noted wryly.

"I'm planning a career in nursing and I'd like to ask you some questions pertaining to that, if it's not too much trouble?"

"Not thinking of nursing on the eastern front are you? Only bad stories coming from there."

She shook her head. "Oh no, I'm only interested in mental health. I have a little bit of hands-on experience. I looked after an uncle who thought he was a lobster."

"Ha!" said Glopp, "we have a pair who think they're magpies—new arrivals, total fruit-loops." He looked her up and down. "Can I buy you a drink?" He gestured to Rosie for two house wines.

Glopp was a stout man with a florid complexion. He wore elaborate printed pink braces over a white shirt, hitched to white breeches. A pink triangle of fabric peeked out of his chest pocket and a foppish pink beret sat beside him on the table. He wore a different coloured ring on each of his stubby fingers and a curl of hair was gelled to his forehead.

"Magpies!" Lucy looked amused. "How does being a magpie manifest as a disorder? My uncle, the lobster, wore red clothes and hid under the bed a lot."

Glopp sighed. "These two have black and white feather costumes, tails and beaks. They oodle-ardle-oo and flap their arms and spout nonsense about tracking fugitives."

"So how do your doctors treat that sort of illness?"

"When the patients get their strength back—they've just been interrogated over at the Patriot Bureau to make sure they're not spies, it may take a couple of weeks for them to recover—they'll get electricity therapy. If that doesn't work, a snip will."

Lucy nodded her head gravely. "Are there no milder treatments for delusional types?"

"Long term rehabilitation costs a small fortune. Who's going to stump up a mountain of talons for that pair?"

Their wines arrived. Lucy took a sip from her glass and wrinkled her nose.

"What stops them from just walking out?"

"They're under lock and key except for the two hours a day each patient spends in the hospital grounds. We strap the at-risk ones like them to a gurney and leave them under the trees. Saves us having guards watching them the whole time."

"So that might be a good quiet time for me to pay you a visit? I'd really like to see how the hospital runs and what nursing entails, if it's at all possible."

Glopp licked his lips and examined his fingernails. "There are rules around hospital visits you know, you could get me in some serious trouble with Dr Flaystik if he finds you sneaking around the place." He scratched his chin. "But if you're serious about wanting to be a nurse you could apply to the hospital for training. I might let Flaystick know I need a new trainee. Nurse Stigg is heavy with child so I need to locate her replacement sooner rather than later."

"Splendid," said Lucy. "I'll apply tomorrow."

"I presume, ahem, you have other clothes… or the means to acquire a more appropriate choice of outfits?"

"Ah," said Lucy, "not really, or at least, not with me. I'm a refugee from the east, whole village razed, escaped in what I was wearing."

"I see. Well, we can't have a pretty thing like you running around in her night clothes can we, especially if you're going to do serious work in our asylum—you'll be mistaken for a patient. Drink up, we only have a few minutes to get our foot in his door before Dussillaux locks up for the day—he's the only couturier in these parts worth squandering talons on."

"But, I have no money…" began Lucy.

Glopp raised a flat hand. "We'll sort that out later. You need accommodation too, can't have you sleeping in the fields, can we?"

Lucy frowned.

"Cheer up girl, luck prostrates itself twice at your feet. I have an unoccupied garrett in my modest manse. It is yours as a temporary sleeping arrangement in exchange for a few trivial domestic duties." He held up his wine glass and grinned, then quaffed its contents. Lucy reluctantly followed suit with hers.

They crossed the square, took to a side street and found themselves in front of Maison de Dussillaux. A young woman in a dress that resembled a cathedral with flying buttresses was shuttering the large display window with a long hooked stick.

"Ho, Muselle! We have a customer to attire, a refugee from the war. Please call upon your father, Dussillaux, to assist."

"At once, Mr Glopp," she replied, scurrying into the store.

The pair followed her in and stood at the counter. Dussillaux, a thin man with greased black hair and a waxed pencil moustache hailed them as he descended the staircase. "Greetings Master Glopp. Mademoiselle," he said, nodding to each. "You're looking sharp as a pin today Glopp, a credit to your profession."

"If only I could convince Flaystik to avail himself of your services, Dussillaux. We do so struggle to hit the right sartorial note in that fashion wasteland on the hill." He held out his hands in a gesture of defeat.

"It is the way of our times, dear sir… and what a dazzling creature you have on your elbow—albeit one reduced to unfashionable pajamas—Miss…?"

"Whatplease, Lucy Whatplease. Just Lucy will do," she curtsied.

"Astute as ever my dear fellow!" said Glopp. "A walking couture disaster! Poor waif fled the eastern front with no opportunity to pack her case. I'm… ahem, taking her under my wing. She needs to be dressed for a career in nursing in the first instance. And as she'll be staying under my roof she requires a modest selection of feminine items in the second."

"That's really not necessary, just a plain dress…" Lucy began to protest and was cut off promptly by a raised finger from Glopp.

Dussillaux snapped his fingers and called Muselle to fetch a tape measure. The girl reeled off various numbers as she zipped around Lucy's frame with the tape.

"Ha! We can dress your ward from the racks," declared Dussillaux smugly. "She's tailored her body to exactly match those of our mannequins. If only more girls were similarly considerate. Jungaputt's oldest daughter Gertmede requires three times the normal length of cloth to embellish her dramatic frame, and Turpile's youngest, Aurora is even more rapacious for silk."

He pulled a plain white smock from a row of dresses. "This one is simple, but made out of the finest Veltijin silks… and note an exotic samite tapestry that runs along the spine. All the rage on the catwalks of Delán. She'll be the envy of your entire seraglio, Glopp!"

Glopp nodded appreciatively. "We'll take two."

"And feminine items?" Dussillaux paused with a finger on his lips in meditation. "I take it you don't plan to attend soirees together—not yet, at least?"

"There is no need for a ball gown," chuckled Glopp. "Underclothes and similar informal apparel for her to wear around the Glopp residence. Make them pretty and lightweight. And perhaps a pair of high shoes. She can shop for your more fashionable items herself when she has a steady income. Far be it for a man like myself, however knowledgeable he may be in the seasonal winds of fashion, to presume to dress a young woman in her street clothes. My taste for shimmering gold leaf would be redundant if her own tastes tilt in the direction of sack cloth."

"Informal apparel. Hmmm. Your preference in these matters veers towards lace and wispy silks if I am not mistaken, Master Glopp?"

"That is correct," he smiled. "She'll perform a few minor household chores for me which I will supervise. It follows that I may need to critique her work and encourage improvements from time to time. I have a reputation for strictness that is not imaginary. But I see no reason to dress her in cheesecloth. Girls are wilful creatures, full of teasing and play. They prefer attire that stimulates and discomforts their masters. Let her embroider her fine haunches in lace if that is her whim. I am unlikely to be demotivated by such caprice."

"Just so," replied Dussillaux. "A well chosen uniform might even enhance the irksome responsibilities of a supervisor. On unrelated matters I have found the riding crop to be a particularly effective critique of shoddy work—we have a new range in stock as part of our equestrian collection if you're interested in such paraphernalia."

❆ ❆ ❆

They made their way via a series of narrow alleyways and steps that led to 13 Swell Hill Lane—a terraced brick house.

"Another refugee journeyed with me from East Falde... he kept me safe from wolves and bandits, a very fine fellow. Would there be any chance of accommodation for him too?" Lucy asked Glopp hopefully.

"None whatsoever," Glopp replied airily.

"Then I should let him know I'm safe."

"Be quick, girl. Cooking our supper is the first of your evening tasks. We do things on time at the Glopp residence."

Lucy left him with their parcels by his front door and marched briskly to the tavern. Pierrot sat on a bench outside looking anxious.

"I have landed a job at the asylum, and devised a partial plan for rescuing the magpies," she told him.

"Clever young kagu," he said, only half relieved.

"There is an unfortunate hitch though... I had to accept Mr Glopp's offer of work clothes, and I'll sleep under his roof and do chores for him. He's in charge of the nursing staff and I can't really say no to him. You and I will have to separate for a few days. Will you be alright? Have you found somewhere to roost?"

"An orchard beyond the city, as you turn up the road toward the hospital. It has a stately oak tree on the high side. I've already started making a nest in the middle branches."

"Good. I'll come and see you in a few days once I'm settled in. We'll discuss the plan when I get a better idea of the hospital layout. You use our food, and buy more if you have to, I don't need it. And stay hidden, no reason to take any risks."

❊ ❊ ❊

Glopp showed her an attic room that would be her lodgings. It had a slanting ceiling and a single window at the end. She had a cot with blankets, a small wooden table and chair, a wardrobe and an oil lamp. He handed her one of the smaller clothes boxes, instructing her to wear its contents and to meet him in the scullery in a few minutes.

Lucy opened the box when Glopp departed. It contained two small pieces of yellow lace lingerie. She shrugged, tossed off her nightdress, put them on and followed him down the stairs.

"Dussillaux has outdone himself this time, the man is a genius!" declared Glopp. He sat on a too-small-for-his-frame wooden stool in the tiny kitchen admiring Lucy's appearance.

"There isn't much of it," she said with a frown.

"Nor should there be," he responded. He placed a hand on her hip and slowly turned her around to view her back. "What a pert bottom you have dear… succulent with more than a touch of insolence, quite perfect! Dussillaux has done me more favours than he has done you. He knows me rather too well," he chuckled.

"Is this some sort of mating dance?" she asked, remembering how Pierrot had behaved bizarrely when she wore his feathers.

"Most definitely not," he said. "Don't get thoughts above your station. The Glopp residence has only one master. It is a place where we do our chores on time and we do them well… you will be diligent and self-disciplined," he added.

He instructed her to stand by the sink and place her hands flat on its surface, then he picked up his new crop and stood behind her. "On the subject of self-discipline, there is also another form of discipline we practice here. I will now demonstrate what happens if you fail to perform your tasks to the expected standard. Accept this as a warning and deterrent."

He swished the crop through the air a few times, adjusted the lower piece of her scant attire to his liking, then tapped her behind to take aim. He proceeded to flick it across her buttocks, a dozen stinging strokes. She caught her breath after the first stroke, thereafter making no further sounds.

"You can prepare vegetable soup now," he said breathily. "Your ingredients are on the bench beside the stove, as are utensils and chopping boards. Do not turn around or face me unless you want twelve more."

Glopp returned to the stool at the back of the scullery. Lucy slowly began chopping the root vegetables. Her knife was heavy and sharp and, wiping a tear from her eye, she entertained uncharacteristically dark thoughts, but calmed herself down and put them aside. Behind her she heard scuffing sounds and a rhythm of heavy breathing that reached a crescendo and abated.

✽ ✽ ✽

"You are extremely fortunate, girl. Today you'll see our eminent Dr Flaystik demonstrate the use of seizure therapy as a primary treatment for patients suffering depression. These demonstrations are normally for senior medical staff and visiting clinicians, but you were curious about the range of treatments we provide so as a special favour I thought to include you today. Do not speak or ask questions and pay respectful attention. Dr Flaystik is widely renowned for his use of chemical, electrical and surgical remedies to treat the mentally ill."

Glopp scanned the room and nodded to various of his colleagues. He was notably deferential towards his superiors and in equal measure dismissive of his underlings.

They sat together in the front row. Lucy had been undergoing nurse training at the hospital for five days and was already well liked by staff and patients. She was diligent and uncomplaining carrying out her assignments, and kindly disposed towards patients—therefore considered perhaps a little too sweet natured by certain senior staff members who maintained emotional detachment was desirable and largely impossible without a grain or two of truculence.

Glopp aligned with that opinion. He was puzzled that she appeared to engage a full emotional spectrum with patients yet remained aloof and detached in their nightly entertainments. It was, he decided, only a small annoyance. He had some exciting innovations planned around a birch for this very evening that were certain to undo her cool passivity.

Flaystik entered the auditorium and addressed the audience without ceremony.

"Today's demonstration is on the administration and benefits of a stimulant medication developed in this very hospital and registered as Flaystik's Tincture. It induces seizures in the patient—similar to electricity therapy—which have the primary effect of pacifying and flattening out emotive responses. The convulsions you'll witness today are produced by an intense stimulation of the vegetative and motor centres of the brain stem. This leads to drastic alterations in the patient's internal environment."

Flaystik paused and scanned his audience, raising his eyebrows and cocking his head when he noticed Lucy. He said in her direction "If you are squeamish, I suggest you leave the room now…"

Lucy ignored his invitation and he continued.

"Fear and panic normally accompany seizure therapy. This is due to sensations experienced by the patient in the time between the injection of the drug and the onset of convulsion. Patients complain the sensations are like a crushing of the chest, electrocution, bursting open of the head and dying. These sensations tend to cause histrionics. It's important that the physician is not tempted by all the commotion to suspend treatment prematurely."

He smiled. "Seizures begin roughly a minute after the patient receives an injection and can result in fractured bones, torn muscles and other minor adverse effects. There's a 4.7% mortality rate, which I'm sure you'll agree is a modest risk given the benefits attached to successful treatment."

A patient strapped to a gurney was wheeled into the auditorium along with a tray table that had gloves, bottles, syringes, a mask and other surgical paraphernalia.

"I'll remove his gag after the injection," Flaystik explained in an aside. "Patients in his situation tend to beg which is both demeaning and distracting, but his reaction to the tincture and during convulsion is worth observing."

A group of six patients strapped into wheelchairs who were placed in a half circle on the hospital lawn grimaced in unison as the screaming started. It continued unabated for four minutes and then faded away. Five had been crying when the orderlies came to collect them, the sixth was catatonic.

❆ ❆ ❆

Lucy said nothing but a perfunctory yes or no for the rest of the day. She mulled over the demonstration and the casual cruelty with which it was conducted and the underlying purpose of the asylum.

She was aware that among the inmates, some had been admitted for having nothing more than delightful eccentricities, the magpies among them. A few were committed for being sceptical about things that people take for granted. Lucy felt she would likely be classified in this group if she gave voice to her observations more often. Another type could not comprehend the social rules of the culture they were in. Pierrot would be grouped with them were he to remain in Falde. And some at the asylum were truly tormented. But none of the patients seemed as dangerously mad as people beyond the asylum walls—in the spoiled lands of East Falde, or as dangerously mad as those running the asylum.

Glopp's domestic cruelty echoed a pattern she saw in the asylum, of misery wearing a varnished mask of necessity or authority, masquerading as compassion.

Dr Flaystik was, she believed, more diabolical and more subtle in his twisted pleasures. He appeared to delight in treatments that drew screams from patients, documenting in minute detail their physical and emotional responses to his tortures—classifying their fears, desires and anxieties with an eye to publishing his observations and enhancing his medical reputation.

The magpies were not the only ones who needed rescuing from this terrible place. It was too late for many of the poor souls who shuffled around expressionlessly, but what of the queue of patients who waited to join them? Why were their carers not appalled by this procession?

Against such a panoply of horrors, the preening, arm flapping and squawking of Birdlanders, their silly parades, contests and festivals, seemed charming and eminently sane.

7 | Escape

On the ninth day of her training Lucy was instructed to run a small hospital errand to town. She made a diversion and paid a visit to Muselle at Maison de Dussillaux asserting that Master Glopp had petitioned his superiors to consider Dussillaux as the hospital's new couturier. She requested samples suitable for use by male orderlies, theatre assistants and nurse-aids. These she dropped off at Pierrot's nest along with a memo written on hospital stationary and a badge she had crafted that read 'Deaf and Mute, please use Sign Language'.

The magpies, she told him, would be strong enough for treatment in two days—the rescue would be tomorrow. They pored over the details of her plan and she left him to prepare his role.

Pierrot took the road east from Upper Swell. After a few hours he reached the fork off the main road that led him down a rutted lane. Locating their aircraft he removed the balloons, detached the rudder and wings, tied the satchel with their plumage and guy-ropes to the handlebars, and rode back to his nest.

He spent the afternoon practising a nonsense version of sign language that Lucy had shown him. He was glad to have tasks to do. Lucy was his compass in this strange land and their prolonged separation caused him anxiety. He worried about her too, that her mood had changed noticeably over her three visits to his nest. She was becoming introspective and joyless.

❊ ❊ ❊

Lucy met Pierrot at the gate and walked him to the reception desk.

"I believe you have an identity tag for Mr Flaystik, our new orderly?" she said to the efficient young woman behind the counter.

"Flaystik?" the receptionist asked, surprised.

"Dr Flaystik's cousin, from East Falde. He's a Doctor too," Lucy lowered her voice dramatically, "he had an accident, got too close to a landmine, deaf and mute and possibly some minor brain damage. Dr Flaystik arranged for him to join the orderlies here. You have a badge don't you?"

The receptionist looked flustered. "No, I don't, no one said…"

Lucy held up her hand. "I can assist, he has a copy of the memo."

She turned to Pierrot and waved her hands around in their sign language. Pierrot nodded and produced the letter from his pocket which Lucy handed to the receptionist. It was an authority signed by Dr Flaystik. She skimmed it and handed it back.

"I'm so sorry, there's been a breakdown in communication, I don't have an ID for him."

"Can we make a temporary one until the proper one is printed?"

"Yes, yes of course." She handed Lucy a blank official ID sticker and asked her to fill in his name. Lucy wrote 'Pierrot Flaystik, Orderly' and placed it on his lapel. She gave the pen back with a smile and led Pierrot to the staff corridor.

A group of orderlies were milling around outside the staff room, waiting for their assignments. Lucy introduced Pierrot to them, explaining that he could only communicate in sign language—whispering that they might want to be a little bit cautious around him as he was, after all, Flaystik's cousin.

She made a rapid set of gestures to Pierrot who signed back.

7 | Escape

"I asked him to stay with you gentlemen, he'll help you wheel the patients around."

She left Pierrot and hurried back to her ward where Glopp was waiting for her.

"I have a wonderful surprise for you," said Glopp. "A theatre nurse has taken ill, you will replace her in the theatre today. There are two operations scheduled."

Lucy's eyes went wide. "Two?" she said numbly.

"Dr Flaystik will administer the anaesthetics. Your job is to then put masks on the patients, shave their heads, move their gurneys into theatre and get them ready for Dr Spectre who will perform the surgeries."

"Two?" she repeated, her mind spinning.

"Two, yes," said Glopp, "Our mad magpies. Dr Flaystik has decided to pass on electricity and go straight to surgery with them."

She digested this unexpected twist. "When are the operations?" she asked curtly.

"They start prepping shortly, you should head down there now."

She turned on her heel to leave.

"Oh and Lucy…" he said softly.

She paused with her back to him.

"I think we might take some wrist and ankle restraints home with us tonight. I have devised another innovation I'd like to experiment with."

She made no acknowledgement and walked out the door, turning left for the surgical ward.

※ ※ ※

Dr Flaystik inserted a needle into a small bottle of anaesthetic. He drew the liquid into the syringe and gave it a little squirt to remove the air, placing it on the metal table next to another filled syringe.

"This is your first operation?" inquired Flaystik.

"Yes Doctor."

"Before you came to work here you tried to visit these two didn't you? It's fitting that you get to say goodbye to them. Don't you think?"

"Goodbye?" she asked.

"Well, goodbye to them as mad birds. They won't know who they are after a frontal snip." He chuckled.

The double door swung open and an orderly pushed a gurney into the prep room. He wheeled it over to Flaystik, departing as the next gurney was wheeled in. The magpies were restrained on their stretchers with belts across their chests and around their wrists and ankles. They looked much worse for wear since Lucy had last seen them and were only semi-conscious.

Flaystik glanced at the second orderly and held up his hand. "Hey! You there!"

Pierrot stopped in his tracks.

"Who are you? You look familiar."

He walked up to Pierrot and looked at his ID.

"Flaystik!" he announced. "What! What's going on here?"

Pierrot pointed at his sign language badge and made some unconvincing hand motions.

"You were that fellow who came here in a nightgown, with the trainee nurse…"

A sudden sting in his buttock was followed by a rush of cool fluid. He turned to see Lucy holding a syringe. His eyes went wide.

"Oops," she said.

"You little vixen!" he cried.

"You seem to have backed onto a syringe. How careless of you, Dr Flaystik."

Flaystik stumbled, and grabbed the edge of the nearest gurney. He crumpled slowly to the floor.

The door swung open and Glopp walked in.

"Is Dr Flaystik around?" he asked Lucy. "There seems to be a kerfuffle about some new orderly claiming to be his brother or cousin…"

"Help," yelped Lucy, cutting him off mid-sentence, "the doctor slipped and fell, he needs assistance!"

Glopp scurried over and bent down to examine the Doctor. He felt a sharp sting in his buttock. He looked confused for a few moments, then slowly crumpled on top of the doctor.

Pierrot stared at Lucy with his mouth open.

She smiled at him. "They're just sleeping Pierrot, they'll be fine, but we need to dress them as patients to buy time for our escape. When these two wake up, it's going to get a lot harder to get away.

7 | Escape

Can you fetch two more gurneys from the corridor please?"

Lucy and Pierrot worked quickly to get Flaystik and Glopp into gowns and onto the gurneys. It was no small exertion, both were dead weights and Glopp was particularly heavy. Lucy shaved their heads roughly, put surgical masks on them and wheeled them into theatre, satisfied they were unrecognisable to any cursory inspection.

She went to the cupboard and emptied a half dozen bottles of anaesthetic and a handful of syringes into a medical pouch then loaded four additional syringes with fluid. She gave the magpies a jab each to keep them quiet, then a half jab to the men in the theatre to prolong their sleep. She tucked the fourth into her pouch for emergency use. Confusion and a lack of hospital leadership would be their allies. The surgeon and his team would arrive soon. It was time to spirit the magpies away.

With a gurney each, Lucy led Pierrot down the service corridor to the loading bay. A laundry van making a delivery of towels and sheets was backed up to the dock with no sign of the driver.

"Change of plan, Pierrot!" she said. "We'll load them in the back of that van, you get in with them."

A short time later a bearded man with flaming ginger hair, and a swaggering twirled moustache emerged from the corridor.

"Excuse me," asked Lucy, "are you driving back to Upper Swell?"

"That I am," replied the driver.

"Would it be possible to catch a ride? I'm late for an appointment."

The driver grinned toothily. "No skin off my nose. You're new here aren't you?"

"My second week," she said, climbing into the passenger seat. "I'm Lucy by the way."

She watched him carefully as he started the engine, put the van into gear and released the handbrake.

"Mullet," he introduced himself. "Good to see some new blood around the place. Where are you living?"

"I have lodgings with Mr Glopp," she said.

He glanced at her with an eye swivel and grimaced. "My condolences. Old Glopp has a reputation in Upper Swell, but you'd know what I mean better than me if you're sleeping under his roof."

"A reputation? I can't imagine that. He's been very sweet to me…

oh, what was that noise?"

"Noise?" enquired Mullet.

"Is there someone in the back of the van? I heard some banging?"

Mullet stopped the van just outside the hospital gate. He slipped the gear stick into neutral, pulled the handbrake on and got out to have a look. Opening the back door he was greeted by the unexpected sight of Pierrot sitting between the two gurneys.

"What the…" he was interrupted mid exclamation by a sting in his buttock. He turned to see Lucy discarding a syringe.

"I'm truly sorry, Mullet, it's nothing personal. You'll sleep for a few hours, but you'll be fine. I need to borrow your van, is all. Oh, and by the way," she said, as he crumpled to the ground, "you were right about Glopp."

Pierrot retrieved the tandem from its hiding place under some brambles by the gate. He placed the bike and satchels in the back with the magpies then climbed into the passenger seat. Lucy took the wheel.

"You know how to control this thing, young kagu?" gasped Pierrot, his eyes like saucers.

"We'll find out."

She released the brake, clutched the motor into gear and applied light pressure to the accelerator, imitating Mullet. The van pulled out rather too smoothly. She suspected that she might have done this before.

At the bottom of the hill they turned east, in the direction of the Falde Coast.

❄ ❄ ❄

"Is there any chance the doctor and your landlord have had the surgery that was intended for our passengers?" Pierrot sounded worried. "The brain surgeon might not have checked their identities."

"I hope not, Pierrot. I wouldn't wish that operation on anyone. But if they did go under the knife… perhaps Dr Flaystik's replacement will be less likely to use convulsants and scalpels as preferred treatments. It might be quite a good thing for the patients. And Glopp with a snip can only be a better person."

7 | Escape

Pierrot stared at Lucy intently. "Is there anything you want to tell me? About Glopp?"

"Not really, Pierrot. He has cruel pleasures—there were nightly beatings—but he didn't hurt me because I didn't let him. Glopp saw my apparent destitution as an opportunity. But I deceived and exploited him too, to get into the hospital. It was a trade."

She went quiet for a minute. "Anyway, let's hope he and Flaystik are both coming out of their stupor now without the bandages."

Pierrot thought about that for a while.

"You exploited him to save those two in the back. It's not really a trade, Lucy, more a sacrifice."

She stared ahead and said nothing.

"Though you do seem very proficient with those needles. I hope you don't find a reason to put me to sleep."

Lucy giggled. "Watch out Pierrot, I've had an entire week of medical training!"

They drove on in silence for another hour.

"Do you think they're chasing us, Lucy?"

She smiled. "This van was an incredible stroke of luck. We'd still be evading them on two wheels. We've been driving on this road east for at least three hours. The authorities won't risk this direction for too long."

"Do you have a plan for when we get to the coast?" he asked.

"Yes. The plan is that we try to find a boat. There might be some abandoned vessels in a war zone or an opportunity to borrow something. Then we work out how to sail... then we try to navigate due east and we cross our fingers that it's the right direction."

"Ah," said Pierrot. "And do you have enough anaesthetic to keep the magpies quiet. They might have other ideas."

"I'm hoping that we can reason with them. Or if we can't, that we can trick them into cooperating. Needles are my emergency resort."

The van coughed and spluttered. The engine cut out and it rolled to a stop.

"I guess we're back to Plan A—peddle power," said Lucy, climbing out of the van.

"What's that smell?" asked Pierrot, sniffing and wrinkling his nose.

"War, Pierrot. That's the smell of war."

❄ ❄ ❄

The magpies had been awake for some time, squawking and complaining. Their gurneys were strung in single file behind the tandem, tied nose to tail, and it was slow progress. The eastern road began to wind up a hill that had looked daunting enough in the distance. Now it seemed that it would take an impossible effort to get beyond its gentle lower slopes. Lucy signalled Pierrot to pull over.

"I think it's time to negotiate," she told Pierrot.

She snapped down the gurney wheel locks, said, "do either of you magpies understand where you are, who we are, and what has happened to you in the last two weeks?"

"Untie us you beast," said one.

"You have no right to do this to us. We're on official magpie business," chimed the other.

Pierrot moved to stand next to Lucy. He addressed the magpies, first one, then the other. "This is Lucy," he said, placing a hand on her shoulder. "Lucy Whatplease. She's the yellow spotted kagu you've been chasing. She knew you were chasing her and that you meant her harm, but she saw that you were in trouble and insisted on saving you anyway."

The slightly bigger magpie looked from Pierrot to Lucy and back. "She's not a yellow spotted kagu… and who are you? I don't know you."

"She's in disguise. So am I." Pierrot paused for a few moments. "You were captured by some people who weren't very nice. They tortured you. Then they healed you just so they could give you brain operations. The surgery they were planning would have been worse than the worst torture you can imagine. You would be like dead birds walking. But Lucy planned a daring rescue and executed it at great personal risk."

"You did too Pierrot," Lucy inserted.

"No. I would have left them there without worrying about what happened to them, Lucy. It's you that these two need to thank." He turned back to the magpies. "In order to rescue you, Lucy had to endure some torture as well. Have either of you ever done anything that considerate for a fellow bird? A bird that you don't know? A bird that is chasing you and means you harm?"

The magpies were silent.

"Lucy is trying to take you back to Birdland, where you'll be safe. But Lucy won't be safe there because magpies like you are trying to capture her." He took off his glasses and polished them on his jacket. "The reason they want to capture her is so she can become a museum exhibit because she's such a rare and marvellous bird. She's done nothing wrong and your masters only want to hurt her so they can be famous. Just like those people in Upper Swell when you did nothing wrong."

Pierrot let that sink in. "We can't drag you all the way to Birdland—you have to help us to rescue you. And right now we're stuck on this hill for as long as we have you restrained on stretchers. So your choice is simple. You can cooperate and Lucy will do her best to get you home, or we can leave you here strapped to these hospital gurneys and let the bad people take you back to the asylum. You have some thinking and talking to do. We'll give you a few minutes."

He took Lucy's arm and guided her a distance away from the magpies so they could chatter among themselves.

Lucy gave Pierrot a peck on the cheek. He took her hand and squeezed it.

"The smell of war is getting stronger," he said with a furrowed brow. "I don't understand this world."

"Be prepared for some dreadful sights over this hill, Pierrot. If we get lucky we'll find ourselves in a place where the war has done its worst and moved on. If we're unlucky they'll still be trying to kill each other between us and the coast." She looked at him earnestly. "We don't belong in this place. We have to stay as low as possible and move under cover. Either side that captures us will assume we're working for the other."

Pierrot nodded. They stood in silence holding hands.

"You know magpies better than I do, Pierrot. Will they join us?"

"Magpies respect authority, Lucy. They prefer being ordered over thinking for themselves, but they're not entirely stupid. They're a very argumentative species, tenacious to a fault. But they're loyal. If they accept you as our leader, they'll walk through fire for you. They're fearless too."

"I'm not leadership material, but you are. I was thinking about ways to trick them into coming with us but you jumped straight in and told them the truth. You're wiser than I."

"Nonsense. You understand this world in a way I never will."

"That's what worries me."

"Anyway, tricking them might have been easier on our ears. A magpie as a friend can talk the leg off an ostrich... speaking of which, they've had enough time."

Pierrot wandered back to the gurneys followed by Lucy.

"Untie us..." said one.

"Please," said the other.

Lucy undid the straps of one and then the other. Pierrot watched with concern.

"It's ok, Pierrot," she said. "They're weak. They may not even be able to walk."

The larger magpie managed to sit up and swing his legs over the side. The other remained on his back after a failed attempt at sitting.

"What are your names?" asked Lucy.

"Pica," said the smaller.

"Cissa," said Cissa. He looked at Pierrot. "If she's the yellow spotted myna, then who are you?"

"I'm the Passport Issuing Officer for Upper Birdland, Lower Birdland and the Passerine Peninsula. My name is Pierrot."

"No you're not. That quarrelsome customs fellow is a kagu."

"I took off my plumage."

Cissa looked shocked. "Why would *anyone* do that?"

"Because it's not safe to wear plumage in Falde. You were arrested and tortured because of your plumage."

"What sort of monster tortures you because of your plumage?" asked Pica.

"You two want to take Lucy back so that she can be turned into a Type Specimen because of her plumage. You should ask the birds you work for that very question."

"How do we know you are who you say you are?" asked Cissa.

"Why would we lie? Given that your job is to capture Lucy, it benefits us if you don't know who we are!" said Pierrot.

Lucy walked to the tandem and opened the satchel tied to the handlebar. She removed her dress and put on her yellow spotted plumage. There was a long silence.

"Oh my," said Cissa.

"Oh my," said Pica.

"Oh my," said Pierrot.

"You're under arrest," said Pica.

"No she isn't." Cissa hissed at his companion. "We don't work for the academy now, Pica."

Pica looked perplexed. "Then…who do we work for?"

"I'll follow you," Cissa turned to Lucy. "Even though you're a kagu. If we get back to Birdland, I'll stand at your door and turn away other magpies."

"We," said Pica. "We'll stand at your door."

"*If* we get back to Birdland," Lucy echoed back to them. "You both need some time to recover. You're not fit to trek across land. We have to be furtive and agile on the next leg of our journey. We're entering a war zone over that hill. You'll need to build strength for that."

She went back to the bike and swapped her plumage for the dress. Pierrot loomed behind her.

"The marks…" he asked softly, "around your tailfan? Why were you beaten that way?"

"It had something to do with my plumage, Pierrot," replied Lucy. "Glopp was quite fussy about it. I don't seem to be safe in any plumage."

"I'll stand at your door too," he murmured.

8 | War

They found an overhang beneath a rocky outcrop to hide their wheeled contraptions and deposit the magpies. Exploring a belt of sycamore trees that ran adjacent to the road, Pierrot and Lucy stumbled into a clearing where an ancient Moreton Bay fig swept out in a huge ring of horizontal branches and fluted roots. Pierrot immediately set about making nests in the crooks of its lower branches. Lucy guided the magpies to their new camp then went foraging for wild berries, apples and amaranth seeds to assemble their supper.

Four days passed at their camp without incident. A single vehicle was heard rattling along the eastern road, but there were no other signs of human life to cause concern. With their health returning the magpies lived up to their reputation for chatter, commenting at great length and continuously on their various likes and dislikes. Kagus were surprisingly high on the second list. Pierrot found himself reminding them that he and Lucy were kagus and perhaps other topics of conversation might be considered less delicate.

On the fifth day of their camp Lucy and Cissa hiked to the top of the hill to survey the lay of the lands beyond. Around noon they crested the saddle and encountered a stark and shocking contrast to the verdant greenery of their climb. The hill they stood on was part of a semi-circular chain that created a giant amphitheatre around a bruised landscape, a green frame on a besmirched canvas.

Fields of crops and swathes of trees had been razed or sundered, some were still smoking. Fences were smashed. Cottages were in ruin. Farmlands were empty of animals. A taint of smoke mingled with cooked meats. Rot and raw sewerage drifted on the breeze. The eastern road they had been following disappeared in a few places across the plain, where it had been smashed by war machines or buried in mud slides from breaches in the flood banks of a wide central river. Lucy stared for a long time, calculating where they might detour around the various obstacles she could see. She decided the river itself presented their best path through the devastation.

Cissa stared at the scene in horror. "The forests," he said. "Who would do that to trees?"

❉ ❉ ❉

By mid afternoon they were back in camp. Lucy set out a plan for the journey ahead. They would move onto the plain cautiously. They had little choice about that anyway as Pica was still stiff and using a stick to walk.

Pierrot watched his careful movements with concern.

"What did they do to you two at the Patriot Bureau?"

"They threatened us with horrible things if we didn't tell the truth," said Cissa.

"Told them the truth all along, of course, thought they'd respect the badge, comrades in uniform," added Pica.

"They put cloth over our faces and poured water on them." Cissa scratched his head. "Meant to be a torture I think but... I like a birdbath, didn't mind that at all."

"I enjoyed it too," agreed Pica.

"We had to stand on some cables with electricity in them," Cissa smiled. "Very partial to that. Always enjoy perching on powerlines."

Pica nodded. "They weren't happy. Opposite in fact. Unhappy."

"The next thing was a bit unpleasant…" Cissa looked down at his midriff, "Won't be breeding this season."

"Or next," added Pica.

"Overall though, bit of a relief really, all that preening and wooing and nest building for two seconds of madness."

"Won't miss it either," agreed Pica.

"The guards were… *very unhappy* by then. That's when they got really nasty." Cissa shuddered. "Plucked my beautiful tail feathers… one… by… one… by… one…"

Pica looked at the ground and shook his head. "I screamed and screamed," he said.

Pierrot winced. "You poor birds," he whispered with an ashen face.

Lucy put her hand on Pierrot's knee. "I didn't realise…how hard it was for you to take off your plumage. I'm sorry."

Pierrot put his hand on hers, shrugged. "Don't be. You were exactly right."

"This is no place for birds," she said softly.

"But why is that?" asked Cissa. "They have trees here too."

"Falde, the people here, they don't want you to have an identity that isn't their identity. You're only safe when you dress like them and talk like them and act like them. You're outsiders here, aliens—they fear outsiders."

"Why are these people so different to Birdlanders?" asked Pica.

"Are they?" Lucy shrugged. "Maybe people are all the same and you have to be an outsider to see it… tell me, Pica, are there any people who aren't birds in Birdland?"

"Of course there aren't!" said Pica. "Everyone's a bird in Birdland."

Lucy half-smiled and nodded.

Pierrot took off his glasses and massaged the bridge of his nose. He nodded too and said, "Perhaps you have to be an outsider, or someone with no memory of how things were to see how things are."

❊ ❊ ❊

Pica managed the hill climb with stoic determination. They rested under the brow of the hill for a few minutes. Pierrot sat with Lucy staring at the broken land.

She wore a grim expression. "I can't see any signs of life anywhere. I suppose that's good for us."

"Are you worried about what might be waiting for you there? Or in Birdland, when we get home?" asked Pierrot.

She looked at Pierrot. "East Falde worries me much more. I'm starting to get these fragments of memory. Disconnected. I can't make any sense out of them. I think something bad happened. That plain, it fills me with dread."

Pierrot looked at her sharply.

"You've been here before?"

"I don't know. It's possible. Or maybe it's just the theme of destruction I remember. I get these flashes of things that happened and… I wonder if I'm better off not knowing my past."

"If you want to talk about it…"

"We better get the magpies moving, Pierrot. The emptiness down there might be very temporary."

❋ ❋ ❋

The sun was low on the hills, sending golden shafts across the plain.

At the junction where the river slithered its way between the hills and emerged onto the plain, a mill with a waterwheel lay in smoking ruins. A barge that had largely escaped the destruction visited on the mill hung on its ropes from a guide cable near the centre of the current. It was peppered with holes above the waterline, as though it had been used for target practice, but it was still afloat.

"That would be a handy way to get down river," said Pierrot, nodding at the vessel, "if we could reach it."

"Better than handy," replied Lucy. "Can you hand me two guy-ropes from the bag."

Pierrot pulled them from his satchel. "What are you planning? These ropes are too short to be of any use."

She stared at the craft and its mooring lines. "Find a pair of sticks to use as barge poles, Pierrot."

The ferry's guide cable was attached to a heavy eyebolt anchored at the crown of a large boulder, a dozen metres back from the riverbank and similarly fixed across the river. Lucy scaled the boulder. She secured a loose loop around the cable with one end of a rope and tied the other end around her waist. She did the same with the second rope, then she pushed off from the boulder so that she was hanging directly under the cable.

Supporting all her weight on the back rope, she advanced the front loop most of a metre, then transferred her weight to that rope to slide the back loop forward. By this system she propelled herself in steps towards the barge.

Her companions watched her from the riverbank in the dying rays of the sun. Its golden light was soon replaced by spectral moonlight reflecting blue off the water.

"Kagus are far more resourceful than I realised," observed Cissa.

"Who knew?" said Pica.

Pierrot shook his head in wonder.

❉ ❉ ❉

The winch sprang to life and the vessel began moving. Lucy heaved a corpse that was draped over the taffrail into the water. The woman had been shot multiple times trying to escape the fate of the mill. Her corpse was less than two days old. Holes on both sides of the barge suggested she was forced by circumstance to park the boat in the middle, caught in a crossfire.

Pierrot and the magpies waded out to the barge when it halted in the shallows. Pierrot had fashioned two long poles from stout saplings which he passed up to Lucy before clambering aboard. She reversed the winch and they moved back to the main current.

"We glide under cover of darkness," she advised them. "We need a pole on either side of the barge to keep us away from shallows. We can take turns and maybe steal some sleep in between. There's a full moon tonight. No one talks or makes any noise and we stay low, silent running, no silhouettes—this boat is flotsam to anyone who sees it from the bank. Understood?"

They murmured their assent.

"We're in a swift current so we should cover a good distance towards the coast. Pica and I have the first shift on the poles. You two find somewhere to rest on deck. We have to be ready to abandon the barge at a moment's notice so keep the bags nearby, Pierrot."

Lucy unhitched the ropes and winch line and the barge slid away on the current.

❊ ❊ ❊

The first night watch for both pairs was uneventful. On her second shift Lucy saw dark figures on the northern riverbank moving to keep up with the barge. They were halted by brambles and thorns that formed a barricade at the river's edge. An hour later she saw furtive figures on the south bank. Thereafter she stayed alert, waking only one companion to join her per shift

As dawn began to smear a faint glow on the horizon they arrived at a major bend in the river, its course turning away from the edge of the plain towards the centre of the devastation. Lucy and Pierrot poled the barge into the shallows where it came to rest. Nearby a hamlet had been razed, its outer walls reduced to piles of rubble, its houses a collection of broken masonry and charcoaled timbers. It was the only place in the vicinity where they were likely to find shelter. A neighbouring forest was black, smoking and uninhabitable.

"Perhaps we'll find an intact basement or structure in that town to stay out of sight."

Pierrot nodded. "So where did you learn that trick with the ropes?" he asked.

"I've absolutely no idea. Let's rouse the magpies shall we?"

She tapped Cissa on the shoulder and went to do the same to Pica, but saw his eyes were already wide open with a look of alarm.

"There's someone else on this barge," hissed Pica, "below deck!"

Lucy put a finger to her lips and held up a hand. She moved stealthily to the hatch and hovered over it with her eyes firmly closed, covered with her arm to acclimatise to the dark below. She slid the hatch back and looked inside. A little girl cuddling a soft toy looked back at her in panic.

"Hiya!" Lucy said in her friendliest voice, "My name's Lucy. What's yours?"

"Lucy," said the girl.

"Yes that's my name. Oooh, what's your friend's name?" she asked, indicating the toy.

The girl squeezed it tight to her chest.

"Georgie," she said.

"Is he a bear?"

"Georgie's a dog."

"Of course he is, it's so hard to see in the dark. Can I come down and join you please?"

"Help my mum," said the little girl. "Please. She's very sick."

"Is you're mum on deck?"

"Yes."

"I need to come down first, ok?"

Lucy climbed down and sat next to the girl. She put her arm around her. "You were going to tell me your name?"

"Lucy."

"Lucy? Well that's easy to remember! It was very brave of you to hide down here, Lucy. It must have been very scary."

Little Lucy pursed her lips and nodded.

"Your mum was brave too, very very brave. She saved your life. You saw her on deck didn't you?"

"She's sick... I couldn't wake her..."

Lucy squeezed her and said, "I'm so very sorry, Lucy. Your mum isn't going to wake up. Where's dad?"

There was a long numbed silence. Little Lucy pressed herself against Lucy. Her voice trembled as she spoke. "They took him away to be in the army."

"I'm going to look after you now, Lucy," she said. "Do you understand? I'm your friend now and no one will hurt you."

Pierrot's head appeared at the hatch. He squinted into the hold.

"There are five of us now, Pierrot... six. Lucy and Georgie are joining us. We can't stay here on this barge. Tell Cissa and Pika to scout the town and find a place for us to hide. Tell them to be quiet, stay low and avoid anyone they see. You stay here with us. I need your eyes on deck. If you see anyone who isn't a magpie, bang on the hatch and pole us out of the shallows."

He disappeared.

"My friends and I are playing a bird game, Lucy. Two of them, Cissa and Pika, are magpies. Pierrot, who I was just talking to, is a kagu—that's an exotic tropical bird—and so am I. What sort of bird do you want to be, Lucy? A Magpie? A kagu? Or a myna? Or a sparrow? Or something else?"

"A myna."

"Oooo! Yes!! You look just like a myna. A very good choice. And shall we make Georgie a bird too?"

"He's a dog, silly."

"Yes, but, you don't think he'd like to dress up with tail feathers and wear a bill?"

She shook her head.

"Well you would know, he's your best friend. I have some yellow plumage for you to wear. It will help you stay warm. It's big—so maybe you can just wear the top half—and it's really meant for a kagu, but we'll pretend it's myna plumage until we can get you proper myna plumage. Ok?"

Little Lucy nodded.

Lucy poked her head out of the hatch and asked Pierrot for the satchel containing their plumage. She dressed little Lucy and brought her up on deck.

"Pierrot, I'd like you to meet Lucy. She's a myna as you can see, and this is her dog Georgie."

Pierrot stared at her for a moment, then he bowed low. "It is an honour to meet you, little myna, and I have long awaited the pleasure of meeting a dog. He looks remarkably like a loon with whom I'm acquainted and that is a great compliment. I am at your service, both."

"Pierrot is especially fond of young mynas. He'll look after you too," Lucy told her. "He's the nicest kagu I know."

She kneeled down to look little Lucy in the eye. "In a few minutes we'll leave this barge, Lucy, it's not safe for us in daylight. The bad men you escaped from and their friends are still around. We need to hide from them. We're heading for the coast to get away, travelling by night. I need you to be a big girl and help us so we can all escape together. We have to be as quiet as possible and we have to put aside all the terrible things that have happened to us for now. You're with friends and you'll be as safe as we can make you."

Little Lucy nodded.

A few minutes later the magpies came darting out of the shadows and across the shallow water to the side of the barge.

"We found a tunnel under a ruin," whispered Cissa.

"It's out of sight, no one around," whispered Pica.

"Good work," Pierrot praised them. "We have two additions to our party." He introduced Lucy and Georgie.

Pierrot and Lucy pushed the barge back into the current where it resumed its downstream voyage. It's only use to them now was as a decoy, Lucy explained. Parked in the shallows it was a calling card.

They made their way to the semi-collapsed tunnel the magpies had found, part of an extensive wine cellar that had collapsed at both ends leaving a small squeeze as its only entrance. There were broken bottles strewn around but a few cases had survived the bombardment that wrecked the village above. A very small amount of light found its way into the cellar through ventilation grills.

Lucy stopped before the entrance and prepared a syringe with anaesthetic. She was the last to go in and she piled broken bricks and fragments of masonry behind her to make the gap smaller and less inviting.

Inside they spoke in whispers. Pierrot distributed food from his satchel. Cissa was posted with the syringe at the entrance and shown how to jab anyone who crawled through the hole. Lucy spent time keeping little Lucy quietly engaged while the other two snoozed, then Pierrot took over with little Lucy so that Lucy could sleep.

There were occasional male voices and other sounds outside and gunfire in the distance. A huge war machine shook the ground as it rumbled by the village, but little else punctured the eerie creaking silence of the town.

In the late afternoon Lucy was awoken by Pika and led to a soldier sleeping soundly just inside the tunnel. She instructed Cissa and Pica to move him a good distance away from their hideout and douse him in wine. They left him with the empty bottles at his feet and propped him against a full case of wine.

She decided against taking his hand weapon. The Birdlanders would get themselves into trouble with guns, especially weapons they weren't familiar with, and she was disturbed by her over-familiarity with this one. Even in the dark she knew the make of the pistol and how to reload its magazine by touch. She prepared another syringe but there were no further incidents.

❈ ❈ ❈

At nightfall they vacated the hideout and made their way back to the river. They headed downstream along its bank, walking in single file with spaces between them. Cissa led, with Lucy behind him, little Lucy riding on Pierrot's shoulders with Georgie sitting on his head and Pica at the rear.

An hour into the walk they encountered the barge in the shallows, snagged on a branch. It was still—remarkably—afloat despite being riddled with holes. They poled it out into the current and were whisked away. Behind them, on the riverbank—close to where they found the barge—Lucy saw men with tracking dogs. She said nothing about it to her companions.

Around midnight the barge slid towards a large town which had some of its buildings still intact. There were lights glowing from a number of windows. They manoeuvred the barge out of the current to consider their next move.

"This boat looks like junk now… maybe we can drift right through them without causing concern?" opined Pierrot.

"Too risky," said Lucy. "It looks like a field camp for one of the factions to me. They won't let something this large float through unchallenged. We have to avoid this town. In fact, we're already too close, there'll be patrols. We need to backtrack and swing a wider arc around it."

"Didn't want to mention it," said Pika, "but I don't think I'd backtrack."

"Did you see people on the bank?" asked Lucy.

"They seemed interested in our boat."

"Which side of the river?"

"This one."

"Damn!" Said Lucy. "If we pole across to the other side, the current puts us in that town. How much time do you think we have before these people get here, Pica?"

"Not much… minutes."

"Town it is," said Lucy.

They pushed back into the current.

❄ ❄ ❄

The river widened and the current lessened. The barge drifted lazily toward the town.

"Whoever runs this town controls our fate now," said Lucy. "We hand ourselves to them as war refugees. If we try to evade capture, they'll kill us for sport. You must tell them the truth, that we're travellers caught up by accident in their conflict. Pierrot, you're guiding a little girl who lost her parents and two magpies who escaped from an asylum in West Falde to a bird sanctuary somewhere near the coast to escape the war. Is that understood?"

"Yes," said Pierrot.

"All three of you *must* look after Lucy and Georgie now, don't let them out of your sight."

They nodded.

"I'm going to disappear but I'll be nearby…"

Pierrot looked at her with alarm.

"Don't worry about me, Pierrot, look after yourselves. I'll find you. I promise."

She went to the side of the boat, slipped silently into the water and was gone.

They poled the barge toward a guardhouse outside the city wall. Two soldiers with weapons came out and Pierrot hailed them.

"Can you help us come ashore please," he called.

"Put your hands on your head, NOW!" shouted a guard.

The magpies complied. Pierrot picked up Lucy and held her up. "I have a child. We have no weapons, we'll do whatever you say." He put her down and told her to stay beside him then put his hands on his head.

They were taken to the guardhouse, searched and questioned, then marched into the city, Pierrot with Lucy in his arms. In a brick building with barricaded windows they were escorted to two makeshift cells, the magpies in one, Pierrot and little Lucy in the other. Guards brandishing automatic weapons stood inside and outside each of the doors. After 20 minutes an officer joined Pierrot and Lucy.

"Perry, is it?" he asked.

"Pierrot. And this is Lucy and her dog is Georgie," Pierrot replied.

"Interesting group… I can't quite work out which of you is the spy. You? Or the two nutjobs next door. Or maybe all of you. We're told the Worker's Militia recruit them young." He looked meaningfully at Lucy.

"We're all birds," said Lucy indignantly. "I'm a myna. Lucy's a kagu."

"That's right, little myna, Lucy's a kagu," said Pierrot sweetly. He turned to his interrogator. "Why would we seek you out and hand ourselves over to you if we were spies?"

"Good question. Very good question. The Royal Falde Expeditionary Force is not generally celebrated for leniency with collaborators or spies. Our interrogation methods are a little crude but very effective. You, of course, will know that, so it all adds to the mystery. Tell me about this bird sanctuary?"

"Well, said Pierrot. It's full of birds. It's called Birdland. It's near the coast but I don't know exactly where."

"We were on the coast two days ago and I don't recall seeing a bird sanctuary there?"

"Perhaps it's off the coast?" offered Pierrot.

"I see. Just so you know, you'll be hearing some screams shortly. I've ordered for your two friends to be interrogated using our more persuasive techniques."

"Oh, poor magpies," said Pierrot, staring at the floor. "They've been interrogated before. Please don't make them stand on electrified cables or do that cloth and water thing, you'll drive them over the edge, they're already too close."

The officer called the guard over and gave him some murmured instructions. He left the room. "Thanks for the tip," he said, grinning. A short time later the soldier returned and took up his position.

"Explain to me again, Perry, your relationship with this child?"

"My name is Pierrot. She's an orphan of the war. I promised Lucy I'd protect her."

"Quite. So who killed her parents? Were they enemies of the state in collaboration with the Militia, executed by our brave boys in self-defence? Or did those treasonous militia barbarians commit a heinous crime against good patriots?"

"What does it matter? She's a child, an orphan."

"It matters quite a lot to me. Even a child has its uses."

"That's the wrong answer, sir," said the guard at the door.

"Keep quiet!" The officer spun around and saw a semi-automatic rifle pointing at his chest.

"The guard you sent out had a small accident. My name's Lucy, just by the way." She flicked off her cap and her hair fell onto her shoulders. "Would you like to put your hands on your head or shall I render one or both of those features redundant? I'm itching to test this weapon."

He stared at her incredulously. "You know you can't get away, this building is crawling with soldiers."

"And yet, I don't look worried. Pierrot, can you go next door and untie Cissa and Pika from their chairs please, I only had time to persuade their captors not to trouble them. And fetch something to tie this one, and a roll of tape if you can find one. And take Lucy with you."

Pierrot held little Lucy's hand and led her from the room.

"Who are you?"

"My name is Lucy. I thought we covered that. Frankly, Captain, I'm disappointed in you. You look like the sort of man who might have a family, perhaps even children, and yet you threaten a small child? What were you before you joined the army? A baker? An accountant? Surely not a doctor?"

"Goran Flegg, captain, serial number 11-645-688."

Lucy smiled. "I'm not interrogating you, Goran. I don't want any information from you at all. I have no interest in your war. What I want is for you to reflect on how easily you have become what you are, and what your family would think of you if they could see you interrogating and torturing prisoners, and how you'd feel if someone just like you was interrogating your family."

Flegg looked at her with narrowed eyes. "If you're planning to tie me up then you're not going to shoot me," he said. "So spare me the lecture, what do you want?"

"They're not mutually exclusive propositions, Goran. Maybe I want to see you twitch in your restraints. Don't think for a second that I value your life. If you behave yourself then I'm going to take you on a little journey. I imagine you're curious about that bird sanctuary Pierrot told you about. Perhaps you'll get to see it. But you need to convince me you deserve that privilege. I can always opt for the kind of *leniency* you offer your prisoners."

"You Militia filth!" he spat.

"Sorry to disappoint you but it doesn't matter to me which side you're on. I don't even dislike you. And I should mention, just so you know, those two magpies would have enjoyed the torture you had planned for them. They're odd like that, fascination with pain, extreme sadomasochists. That's why they were in an asylum. I might assign them to guard you, just for a giggle."

He glared at her.

"So, let's see if you can remember how to take orders, Goran." She paused and stared at him. "We're going to leave this building together. On the way out you'll notice the soldiers on duty here have all been disabled. Sorry about that.

"We're going to take one of the trucks parked outside, I'll drive and you'll take the passenger seat and you'll wave us through the guardhouse. You won't try to alert the guard because one of the magpies will have a gun pointing straight up under your seat. I hope the ride isn't too bumpy, hate for that to go off by mistake. It might not even kill you, imagine that! The other will be itching to put a bullet between the guard's eyes. He just might anyway. My point really is we're going to leave in a truck whether you assist us or not. But you would be doing your guards and your innards a huge favour by respecting my request. Any questions?"

Flegg motioned to speak and Lucy put her hand up to stop him. "That was a rhetorical question, Goran."

Pierrot knocked lightly and entered. "Shall I tie him?"

"Not yet, Pierrot, he's decided he wants to come along with us to the coast. He's quite excited to see Birdland. But bring the ties along, just in case he changes his mind."

Lucy bundled her hair back under her cap. They left the building after stepping over numerous inert bodies and collecting their satchels from a desk on the way out.

Pierrot nudged Lucy. "I thought you only had a few of those syringes left?"

"I do," she said, "Didn't need them. I got a few more of my memories back."

Pierrot looked at her sharply.

"Don't worry. They'll all wake up eventually... I hope."

❋ ❋ ❋

Lucy drove through the night. A few clicks past the final checkpoint they pulled over. Captain Flegg was anaesthetised and moved to the back, his hands and ankles bound. Pierrot and little Lucy joined Lucy in the front seat.

"We should reach the coast by dawn, according to our very helpful passenger," said Lucy.

"I was worried for little Lucy in the interrogation room," said Pierrot, giving her a hug.

"I was worried for Georgie," said little Lucy. "Thank you for rescuing him, Lucy."

She glanced down at her ward, then back to the road. "Keeping a promise isn't always as easy as making a promise, Lucy. I have to confess there was a little bit of hope in that one."

"Why were all those soldiers sleeping?" she asked.

"They wanted to do the right thing," said Pierrot, "they just needed Lucy to tell them what it was."

"We're not out of this yet. We should ditch our weapons. The captain said the coast is held by the Militia, which makes this uniform a little risky too. The soldier I borrowed it from didn't fit my dress—a pity as I had to leave it with him. There's another, thanks to Master Glopp, in one of our satchels, could you find it for me please, Pierrot?"

❋ ❋ ❋

They pulled up at the Militia checkpoint on the hilltop where the road began its winding descent to the fishing village.

"We brought you a present." Lucy smiled through the window at the soldier. Behind him four men in Militia uniforms had their weapons trained on the truck.

"This vehicle, as you see, belongs to the Royalists. It might be handy for a covert mission. We captured one of their officers too, he's in the back."

The soldier motioned for Lucy to get out of the cab. He followed her behind the vehicle where she pulled back the canvas. She pointed at Flegg. "He's unconscious, took a wee head knock. He's a captain."

"Who are these people, and the ones up front?" He pointed his weapon at the magpies.

"These two are new recruits, volunteers. The two up front are the sole survivors of a massacre upriver. They need something to eat and a bed for the night."

"We're not taking refugees."

"They have useful intelligence. I need to talk to the CO here."

Who are you?"

"Classified. One of your boys can drive us down."

He motioned to two of the men. One climbed in the back, the other took the wheel. Lucy squeezed into the cab.

❄ ❄ ❄

"My code name is Lucy," said Lucy.

"I have no knowledge of an operative with that code name," said the major.

"You're a major," she said, "you wouldn't. The two 'magpies' don't pass recruitment in peace time, but this is not that. We need uniforms at the front. The spectacled man and the little girl witnessed something 'interesting' and escaped. The Expeditionary Force wants them dead—very bad PR. Means we want them alive, I'll talk to brass about it. They won't be in your hair for long. That prisoner has a lot of good intelligence on troop movements, positions and assets. I'm sure he's *dying* to share it with you. And I need to get a coded message back to HQ today or tomorrow."

"I see. Who should I contact there with your code name?"

"You have a line open to the top desk?"

"That might take some doing."

"I'm sure you're up to it, Major. Secure that first. Don't use my code name on open lines."

He nodded.

"I want to keep the civilian group with me for now, I need to impress on them that I don't exist. Where can we get them food and soap?"

"Dockside Inn for that, I'll let the mess officer know you're coming. He'll sort it out."

"And with an eye on the future, where might I temporarily requisition a fishing vessel? I'll get HQ to send through the ok before I move on that."

"Local fishermen are working for the Militia now. Troops still need feeding. Find a boat that fits your mission parameters and let me know."

"Very good. I'll scan the wharf. Oh, and major… torture him all you want but keep the prisoner alive, at least until I've spoken to my superior."

※ ※ ※

"Where do you lot hail from then?" The skipper of the *Marlin* took an empty seat at their table. "We don't see new people here. Our employers don't normally let refugees into Skaät."

"Birdland," said Cissa.

"Apart from Lucy," Pica nodded towards the little girl.

"I'm a myna," said Lucy between mouthfuls of porridge.

"A very peckish little myna," observed Pierrot.

"Birdland's just an old sailor's tale. I've spent my life on these waters. I'd know if the bird island was out there."

"I've patrolled the Birdland border for a number of years too and I've never seen a passport from Falde, so there you go I suppose," shrugged Pierrot.

"Escape from a lunatic asylum did we?" he smirked.

"You're well informed," said Cissa.

"News travels fast," agreed Pika.

"That close to a snip," Cissa indicated a small gap between his index finger and thumb.

"Rescued by Lucy," added Pika.

"A yellow spotted myna," said Lucy, drawing attention to her dashing plumage.

The fisherman caught the eye of a companion at another table and tapped the side of his head.

Lucy pulled up a seat and sat next to him.

"Did you find what you were looking for at the dock?" Pierrot asked.

"All good," she smiled back. "Your boat going out today?" she asked the fisherman.

"The *Marlin* goes out every day. Army marches on its stomach."

"Handsome vessel, saw it at the dock, you the skipper?"

He nodded. "Lodergard."

"I'm Lucy," she said, "and I presume you've met my companions."

"I thought she was Lucy," he nodded towards little Lucy.

"She is."

"So you're from Birdland too?" He raised an ironic eyebrow.

"Not on your charts then?"

"It's an old fable, along with mermaids and sea monsters."

"Naturally… How far out are your fishing grounds?"

"Depends on the run. Winter cod season, three days north northeast. We work the Stigland coast from Bafintoor to Frostland. In spring, long line tuna, half a day due east, between Pinnacle Rock and Kasimere Reef."

"Do you know where I can get some charts, Lodergard?"

"We keep them in our wheelhouse, all the skippers do. I won't ask why you're curious."

She smiled.

"Eccentric group you're travelling with?" he glanced at the magpies.

"The war's not been kind to anyone in East Falde."

"True enough. I can't work out why they let your circus through the roadblock."

"Who can resist a yellow spotted myna?" she made a face back at little Lucy who was poking out her tongue and giggling.

"I haven't noticed frivolity as a trait of the Militia."

"Soldiers are people too. Perhaps they have their own little mynas at home? What time does the fleet go out?"

"My crew are meeting at the wharf in an hour. We got in late last night. A few boats will head out before us, most later."

❄ ❄ ❄

They were two hours out of Skaät on an easterly heading when she eased back the throttle. Pursuit was always unlikely but Lucy had interfered with fuel lines on the most likely pursuit vessels, just to be sure. Captain Flegg lay on the deck, his hands and feet bound. He had sea sickness to compound his various pains and woes. The magpies looked a little queasy too. Both leaned on deck rails and stared intently at the swaying horizon.

Pierrot sat in the navigator's chair with little Lucy on his lap. Lucy sat at the helm consulting a chart.

"Why did you bring him, Lucy?" asked little Lucy, pointing through the window at their captive.

"He was going to be hurt by other soldiers, Lucy," she replied. "And I promised I'd look after him after he helped us escape."

"But if he's our friend, why is he tied up?"

"Because he's not really our friend, Lucy. He didn't exactly choose to help us. He might do something unpleasant if we free him now. I'm hoping he'll see things differently sooner rather than later."

"How did you get him out of the complex?" asked Pierrot.

"Same way I got you out. The guards in his cell block are nursing some nasty headaches."

"I don't think I want to know how you do that," he scratched his beakless nose.

"A few days ago I recovered a bunch of memories. I've had special training, Pierrot, and... I truly wish I hadn't. I don't much like the Lucy that needed those skills. The one that has no past might be a better person."

"Who you are now matters more than who you were."

❈ ❈ ❈

The sea became calmer and the sun lit their backs as it arced low in the sky.

"What will we do with Flegg when we land Birdland?" asked Pierrot.

"I'll think of something."

He mulled over her noncommittal answer and shrugged.

"You're sure this is the way to Birdland?" he asked.

"No, Pierrot, I'm not even mildly confident. The fishermen know these waters well and don't know the location of Birdland. That's worrisome but it's also a clue. We flew from the Passerine Peninsula in a westerly direction which obviously puts Birdland in an easterly arc from Skaät. Out past Pinnacle Rock on this heading there's a trail of atolls and reefs. An extensive cluster of reefs near the Benthic Trench is marked as a major shipping hazard and generally avoided. I suspect Birdland's tucked in there, surrounded by coral spikes and shipwrecks. If it isn't, we could be at sea a long time."

❉ ❉ ❉

With the sun hanging low in the sky it was too late to attempt a hazardous reef crossing. They harboured for the night in an atoll lagoon on the edge of the reef cluster. The atoll was uninhabited aside from tortoises, seabirds and land crabs, its lagoon ringed with coconut and birdlime trees.

The breeze died away and the sun dropped quickly. A cloudless sky painted a ceiling of shimmering stars.

Lucy untied Flegg's feet. He was soaked with sea spray and in a foul mood after the day's adventure.

"I don't want to tie you up," she told him, "but threatening you with what I will do to you if you harm any member of this party might be less effective than removing that meal from your menu."

He glared at her.

"And just so you know, I would inflict on you a level of misery that even your torturers would consider inexcusable brutality. By leaving you bound, the point is moot."

She led him, wrists still bound, below deck where Pierrot, Cissa and Pica sat around a table while little Lucy sat on the floor lecturing Georgie that yellow spotted mynas don't normally associate with dogs but she was willing to make an exception for him.

She pulled out a seat for Flegg and one for herself. "Tomorrow there's a chance we'll be in Birdland. We need to talk about that," Lucy addressed the group.

"We'll start with you, Goran," she said. "You didn't ask to come to Birdland so I'm going to give you a choice. You can stay here in this lagoon if you choose—plentiful fish and coconuts to live on. This atoll is listed on the charts as Hadjizer's Atoll, a haven in a storm, so your chances of eventual rescue are better than nil.

"Or you can join us in Birdland. That is a one way trip with no chance of rescue if you don't like it. Being a military man, you'll find the culture a challenge. There's no concept of warfare and you'll be deemed mad if you try to introduce it. Your military training and who you are in Falde are meaningless. Everybody in Birdland—including you—is a bird.

"Choose Birdland and you are exchanging your way of seeing the world for another. Neither is more or less sane than the other, but Falde is considerably more brutal. To acclimatise to Birdland you have to let go of Falde and perhaps regain some of the wonder that you had as a child. You will be starting life again. You have until the morning to decide."

Flegg remained silent, his face set like stone.

"Cissa and Pica, I leave it entirely up to you what you tell your employers. I won't be in any personal danger and I don't need a guard detail but thank you both for your very kind offer. Hopefully your tails will quickly be restored to their former glory.

"And Lucy will need proper myna plumage, Pierrot," she smiled at him.

"Before we land though we have to negotiate some nasty looking reefs. I need you all on deck in the morning to locate a channel and help us steer through any openings we find. If you choose Birdland, Goran, we'll consider you one of us and you can assist too."

※ ※ ※

They motored out of the lagoon at first light. Little Lucy stood at the bow with Georgie; Pierrot was forward on port and Pica forward on starboard. All were on the lookout for a potential passage through the semi-submerged coral daggers that formed the outer reef. Cissa had fallen ill with stomach cramps overnight, remaining in a cot below deck. Flegg, who chose to stay with the company, read the charts in the cabin while Lucy steered.

Just before noon Pica spied a potential passage, calling Pierrot across for confirmation. Lucy craned her neck to see and felt a filleting knife pressed against it.

"She witch," hissed Flegg. "You disgust me. You should have left me on the atoll. After I slit your throat, I'll do the same to the others. Might have some fun with the…"

A sudden sting in his buttock was followed by a rush of cool fluid. Lucy felt him tense and pushed his hand away, the knife clattered on the deck. Flegg crumpled slowly.

"He took his time," said Cissa. "Very cramped in that cupboard, can barely stand. Not keen on this motion either, not a seabird."

Pierrot and Pica burst into the cabin.

"What happened?" cried Pierrot.

"He tried to kill Lucy," said Cissa matter of factly, "but wanted to boast about it first."

Pierrot looked at Flegg and the knife on the deck, the needle in Cissa's hand, then at Lucy. "You knew he'd try that?"

"I hoped he wouldn't, but yes, I did. Poor Cissa has been stuck in that cupboard all morning. Thank you, Cissa."

"But if you knew he would, why did you bring him?" Pierrot pressed.

"He had to choose his own path, Pierrot. I'm not his judge or executioner."

Pierrot looked at the inert Captain. "What do we do with him now?"

"Bind his hands and feet I guess."

"No, I mean in Birdland. He's too dangerous to just let him loose."

"Do you have spare kagu plumage Pierrot? I know you have a drawer full of beaks."

"Yes," he said confused.

"We'll dye a set yellow with white spots for him to wear."

Pierrot's eyes went wide and his jaw dropped. "But…"

"Cissa and Pika can take him to the academy. I think we can dissuade the professors from making him a Type Specimen for the foreseeable future. As he's such a rare and endangered species, perhaps holding him for a captive breeding programme in some sort of secure aviary might be the solution."

Pierrot stared at her for a long while, then he nodded. "Clever little kagu."

9 | Bird Sanctuary

A squiggle of blue hills rose out of the ocean and became imposing as the Marlin slid towards the bay. Pierrot changed into his full plumage which included a beak that little Lucy made for him out of a map cover. They were equally delighted with his appearance.

The beach was in a broad curving bay, golden sand and palm trees along its fringes.

"This is my office, little myna," he said as he helped her out of the boat, carried her across the shallows and placed her on the sand.

"Who's that?" she asked.

He swung around and saw a man sitting at his desk. The man resembled a crane. He was slightly taller and ganglier than Pierrot and decked out in startling white plumage with black wing tips. Pierrot threw his arms in the air with comic indignation and marched to the desk.

"Excuse me," he said, "you're at my desk."

"Passport please," said the crane looking unimpressed.

"I'm The Official Kagu," said Pierrot

importantly. "The Passport Issuing Officer for Upper Birdland, Lower Birdland and the Passerine Peninsula."

The crane looked up at him, then pointed at the sign on the desk. A piece of white tape was stuck over the word KAGU on the OFFISHAL KAGU sign and replaced with 'CRANE'.

"This is an outrage!" exclaimed Pierrot. "I'm away on sabbatical for five minutes and an upstart from customs steals my desk."

"My recalcitrant predecessor," replied the Crane, smoothly, "abandoned his post on this border… oh—is that your boat illegally parked in the bay? I really will need to see your passport."

Pierrot raised himself to his full height, his crest erect. The crane, albeit crestless, followed suit. They began strutting around one another in a symbolic display of territorial aggression, barking and wooping, lifting their wings and bobbing their heads.

"What are they doing?" giggled little Lucy.

"Display of dominance," said Pica.

"Crane doesn't stand a chance," said Cissa. "Kagus are angry little birds."

Lucy sighed. "Welcome to Birdland, Lucy," she said.

❋ ❋ ❋

Pierrot escorted Lucy to Professor Tweet's eyrie on the top branches of the Ornithology Department at the University of Rookery. She was dressed in the graceful plumage of a banded kestrel, one of the more handsome species in a distinguished genus. She wore stylish glasses on her curved beak to add a touch of sophistication. Tweet, a sooty falcon, was clearly affected.

"And who is this spectacular creature, Pierrot?"

"Lucy Wha…" Pierrot was cut off by Lucy.

"Good day, Professor. Miss Luciwa Peregrine," she held out her yellow gloved hand to shake.

The professor held it and bowed low.

"I am your humble servant," he said with conviction. Turning to Pierrot he asked "why has it taken you so long to introduce this majestic *Falco zoniventris* to my office, Pierrot? Have I committed a heinous offence against you to deserve such severe punishment?"

"This is my first visit to Birdland, Professor Tweet. I encountered our mutual friend just today in his official capacity at the border and he has escorted me directly to see you. His actions have been brisk and praiseworthy."

"All is forgiven, Pierrot. And do forgive me—I spoke out of turn, smitten by the loveliness of our guest. May I inquire, Miss Peregrine, in what magical land are birds of your remarkable comeliness considered unexceptional?"

She smiled sweetly. "I hail from the Raptor Range, Professor Tweet, but I'm now a faculty member of the Merlin Academy in the Indigo Archipelago. I'm leading a conservation effort to re-establish communities of rare and critically endangered birds. News reached us that you have a male yellow spotted kagu in your care, is that correct?"

"Remarkable! We only took receipt of this specimen a day ago!"

"It must surely come as no surprise to you, Professor, that a host of academics—myself included—avidly follow your distinguished career from afar."

"Well, I suppose my texts on microtonal dissonance in birdsong harmonics may have reached an informed readership."

"Your examination into the taxonomic structure of subjective experience where you infer that these qualia cannot be explained by mere reference to physical or psychoacoustical properties is a rare and lucid insight, Professor."

Tweet puffed up his chest feathers and closed his eyes for a few seconds.

"Naturally one must credit one's colleagues for pushing one in the direction of novel research as an antidote to their own lacklustre curiosity," he said, attempting to overlay his pride with humility.

"There is no need for such a distinguished scholar to be modest, Professor," said Lucy, without a trace of irony.

"On to the point of my visit. The Merlin Academy also has a yellow spotted kagu in its care—although ours is a mere fledgeling. As you know, Professor, this archaic species was long thought extinct. Its rediscovery has caused quite a stir. Between us we now have two living examples, one of each sex, and we would very much like to start a breeding programme to reestablish the species. Might I inquire as to the condition of your specimen?" she asked.

"He's quite confused, slightly deranged in fact, but in robust physical health," responded Tweet.

"Just so," she nodded. "A tiny gene pool and the stress of near extinction. We find that delusional behaviour is common in that situation. Goodness, we had a giant cassowary who claimed he wasn't even a bird!

"Anyway, I have a proposal for you, Professor Tweet. Our kagu is being kept in a secure aviary—she is far too valuable a bird to risk to the wilds. But she is also far too young to breed. Yours is already breeding age, but as we know, kagus are very long lived. If the University of Rookery would care to collaborate with the Merlin on this long term venture, then as the senior academic and nominal head you would naturally be credited with saving this marvellous species from extinction."

"Rightly so." he said with a nod.

"You would need to house him in a secure aviary for the duration, but that conveniently provides you with the wherewithal to compile an adult behavioural study of this undocumented species, if that is your whim. And, of course, your specimen will die of natural causes before ours, making yours the Type Specimen, and…"

She paused for effect.

"And?" he asked.

"Forgive me if I've acted prematurely. I placed a request with the Avarian Society to rename this species 'Tweet's Kagu'—if that nomenclature is acceptable to you, of course."

"I am very impressed with your academic rigour, Miss Peregrine. If only a similar standard of competence was shared by my Rookery colleagues. You aren't perchance looking for a posting to this university are you? You would attract sponsorship from high places and could expect a stellar career path."

"I'm truly flattered by the compliment, Professor. Perhaps in a year or two I might seek a post-doctoral qualification under your direct tutelage, should such an opportunity ever become available?"

"I will see that it does!"

"I take it then that you accept our proposal, Professor Tweet?"

"We will commence construction of a kagu caging facility

forthwith, Miss Peregrine."

"Your foresight is exceptional, Professor. So often academia is bogged down in red tape. It is truly a pleasure to meet one moored to the mire who transcends the rank and file and acts decisively in the name of science."

"You can credit Pierrot for bringing you to the right office, Miss Peregrine. My colleague Saddleback would have dithered and sought a conference with his paymasters. My colleague Brightfeather would have quibbled and bargained for limelight. On unrelated matters, can I tempt you to join me for dinner at the club this evening? The raptor menu is especially tempting."

10 | Flotsam

She could feel pressure on her back and the tingle of a watery sun on her face. An orange blackness inside her eyelids was the sort where descending luminescent dots jump back to the top when they reach the bottom of your eyes.

She heard footsteps.

"Are you awake, Lucy?"

"Yep," she smiled and sat up, rubbed her eyes and opened them.

Pierrot sat down beside her. Little Lucy was a distance down the beach peering into a large intertidal rock pool with Georgie.

"You remembered everything didn't you? In East Falde? You know exactly who you are."

"Yes."

"Soooo…?"

"I was once someone a lot like little Lucy, filled with fantasy and adventures."

She picked up a chunk of pink coral and turned it around in her fingers.

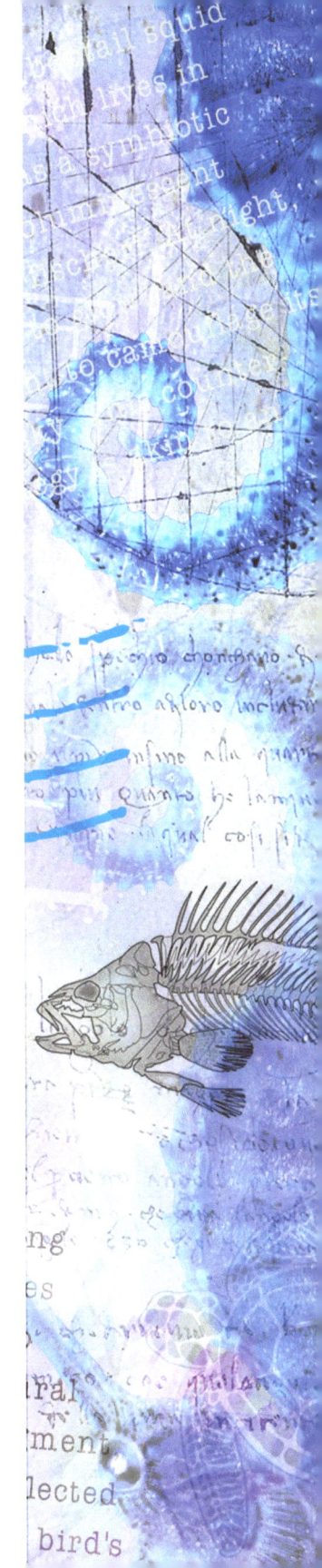

"Growing up is an odd thing, Pierrot. The magic of everyday things slips away, one grain at a time. You don't see it. You fill those little holes with knowledge. There's nothing especially wrong with knowledge, of course, but it has a lot less magic about it than magic."

She held the coral to the light to examine its honeycombed surface.
"And?" he prompted.

"And if you lose track of who you are in the process, maybe you fill up with poorly chosen knowledge and maybe you find yourself using what you know badly. I forgot who I was long before I washed up on this beach. I worked for a common 'good' that wasn't actually all that good, and I became someone who did necessary things, without questioning if they were good things. If you ever have to do a bad thing for a 'good' outcome, that's when you have to question the value of the outcome. I was no different really to those doctors in the asylum or the soldiers in East Falde. If you follow the herd mindlessly, you drink at poisonous waterholes."

"Aannnd?" he prompted again, after a significant pause.

She put down the coral and picked up another, pure white.

"Identity is a funny thing, Pierrot. After all you've been through and seen, are you still certain you're a kagu?"

"Yes. Well, not the same way as before of course. I'm a kagu for as long as little Lucy wants me to be one."

"Birdland was made for Lucy. She loves being a myna. She loves you too. She thinks you're very silly, which of course you are."

"She's a resilient little myna. A joy to have around."

"You two... three—mustn't forget Georgie—are a family now."

"We four."

"You only need one Lucy, Pierrot, the one that needs you."

"So...you're leaving." He took off his glasses and wiped them on a feathercloth. He sighed. "Where will you go?"

"No idea."

He put his glasses back on, then took them off and wiped them again.

"Tell little Lucy not to worry about me. I'll find her again, I promise."

He nodded. "I'll tell her. She knows you keep promises. And me? Will I see you again?"

"You'll see me every day, Pierrot, in little Lucy." She stood up and brushed off the sand. "Walk with me."

Pierrot stood up and they walked along the beach, coming to a small sailboat mostly in the water with just its flat stern sitting on the sand. It had white painted wooden sides and its name *Luciana* was in red paint on the bow. Lucy reached in and retrieved a polkadotted ball, which she handed to Pierrot with a wide smile. She winked at him and climbed in.

"Your call *Luciana*," she said to the boat, which was already slipping into the surf. A gust of wind snapped the sail and the little boat sped out of the bay.

book three

Aves

1 | Ruffled Feathers

From his eyrie in the southwest cupola of the Buzzard Academy, Talon looked down on a rippling carpet of spruce, fir and pine, a confection of dark greens mottled by golden aspen and black larch, spilling haphazardly down the slopes of the Raptor Range. Some distance below, the valley widened into foothills that subsided into Fantail Sweep, a series of lush, broad meadows barely discernible through the blue haze.

Talon's mood was abstracted. The task of preparing speeches to welcome the next intake of fresh-beaked students had fallen again to his agency. His listless colleagues—eager as ever to avoid doing any more than absolutely necessary to maintain their comfortable academic perches—had shunted the responsibility to his inbox.

Professor Talon made a personal point of accepting duties of this sort without enthusiasm or complaint. A gyrfalcon, he would suavely assert, is not cut from the thin feathercloth of a tawny owl or a shoebill stork—not to point the wishbone at anyone in particular, of course.

A rap on the door broke his reverie. Professor Chimango ushered himself in and tossed a journal onto the desk.

"What is this Professor?" queried Talon.

"*Journal of Birdology*, Winter Edition. It's been out for five days."

Talon tilted his head quizzically. "And...?"

"The lead article is about a pair of yellow spotted kagus."

"Never heard of that variant—Rhynochetidae aren't my field. Newly discovered species, I take it?"

"Rediscovered Professor Talon. Long-extinct. Not seen in tens of thousands of years, and now two of them have popped up out of nowhere. Except, they're not nowhere. University of Rookery has taken one under its wing. The Merlin has guardianship of a mysterious other. Merlin are unusually coy about the matter. They're hatching something."

"Oh," said Talon, registering the implications.

"Oh indeed! Already three of the brightest in our new semester enrolments have transferred to Rookery. Make no mistake, this is the tip of the beak. The lure of doing novel research on a living 'extinct' bird will cut through the student intake here and obliterate our post-graduate programme."

"I see."

"Academic staff are convening for an emergency meeting in the dean's eyrie in..." he looked at his breast watch, "fifteen minutes."

❅ ❅ ❅

The ornithology dean, a royal flycatcher with a dramatic red headfan and a mordant disposition scowled at each of the senior educators as they filed into his eyrie. He returned to pecking through his notes, making the summoned professors await his indulgence. When the last of them had been seated for several minutes and all were starting to fidget, he chirped up. "None of this would have arisen if my senior academic staff engaged in the proposed research that landed them their sinecures in the first place!"

It was a typically caustic shot across the beaks from Gizzard-Stone, whose penchant for grumpiness and sarcasm earned him the nickname 'Grizzard the Bustard'.

"We are not all listless!" asserted Tuwoo energetically. "I have an article ready for publication in the *Noxoavis Journal of Owl Parasites!*"

"Professor Tuwoo, your obscure fascination with Dismal Owlbane is commendable but unlikely to inspire a deluge of enrolments at this facility."

"Au contraire," Tuwoo retorted, "Owlbane might be a rare affliction, restricted to a small colony of sandy scops owls, but to any unfortunate animal that hosts *Otusheilonema perstans*, it is not a condition easily dismissed." She scratched behind her ear with a foot, her eyelids squeezed tight in bliss.

"And yet you stated on your stipend application that you are an active researcher in the field of aeronautical wing and tail enhancements, one of the hottest research topics the board has evaluated?"

"Ah, yes, well…"

Gizzard-Stone held up a dismissive wing to halt further discussion on the topic. "The pretexts you have formulated for channelling a handsome stipend into the life cycle of a mythical parasite can be aired at your next performance review Ms Tuwoo. Until then we have important matters to discuss."

Tuwoo scowled and pursed her beak.

Gizzard-Stone continued. "The Merlin Academy runs undergraduate programmes in rare bird conservation and interspecies communications; Rookery has numerous special courses in the bird arts, and a whole department dedicated to aerie engineering and roost mechanics; whereas we have on our programme, let's see… *Bladder Morphology of the Extinct Giant Auk*, *Chromatic Variance in Pea Hen Wing Display*s, and my personal favourite, *A Meta-analysis of Chicken Ground Scratching utilising Heuristic Techniques against a Quotidian Metric.*"

Professor Rouke shifted uncomfortably in his seat, avoiding eye contact with his colleagues.

"And now Merlin and Rookery have both acquired extinct kagus. Why does it feel like the egg on Buzzard Academy's face was laid by its own staff?"

"A yellow spotted kagu is the discovery of a generation, Dean, extraordinary luck. Surely one cannot compete with the vagaries of happenstance?"

"Two of them, Professor Chimango? One at each of our rival institutions?"

"Ah," inserted Talon, "if I may?"

"Don't be coy, Professor Talon, if you have some pearl of wisdom or remedy to alleviate this farce, speak freely."

"The Merlin and the University of Rookery are a considerable distance apart. So…" Talon scanned the faces of his colleagues. "One might reasonably conclude that there is, somewhere, a grouping of this kagu species… a *lost tribe*, out there in the remote reaches," he waved a wingtip. "And two specimens from this collection have found their way into civilisation and been 'discovered'."

Gizzard-Stone stared appraisingly at Talon. "Go on?"

"It follows that there are more of these kagus in the wild, and that we might acquire our own, to balance this apparent luck disparity between academic institutions."

"Acquire *how*, Professor Talon?"

"An expedition, Dean. To the source. Our rivals might have a sole specimen to study but imagine the prestige of discovering an entire no-longer-extinct civilisation? Would we not gain accreditation as the world hub for avapology research and funding?"

When the mutter of comment had dwindled away, Talon concluded. "Such an enormous discovery would be a feather in Buzzard's cap, no?"

"And just how, Professor Talon," queried the Dean, "might one go about locating a lost civilisation, given that it is, as of this minute, lost?"

"An expedition that sets out on a random bearing would be statistically unlikely to encounter success, I agree. But, at least one person knows the correct bearing..."

He let his sentence taper off.

All eyes were on Talon until Chimango broke the silence. "The Merlin Academy claims to hold a juvenile, although we have no independent confirmation of this report, and a juvenile is, anyway, an unreliable homing bird. The individual to whom Professor Talon alludes is the adult male presently under protection at Rookery."

"Precisely!" said Talon.

"And, what you suggest is that we somehow persuade that irascible pedagogue Tweet to grant us an interview with his ward, then persuade the yellow spotted kagu to supply us with the location of his homelands, without alerting anyone's suspicions?" enquired Gizzard-Stone.

"Not quite that..." Talon glanced quickly around the table. "I'm suggesting we mount a *rescue* of their kagu."

"PROFESSOR TALON!" Gizzard-Stone stood up dramatically. "We are a respected academic institution, not a gaggle of feckless geese or a gang of dastardly crows!"

Talon raised an eyebrow. "I am merely pointing at an opportunity to locate the living remnants of a bird species that was lost to antiquity, undoubtedly the greatest avipological discovery of our time. Such an undertaking is advanced wholly in the service of science and for the betterment of all."

He reflected a moment and continued. "Naturally one uses whatever methods one has at one's disposal in an undertaking of this sort. The goal is all important. And if, through its sponsorship of the programme the reputation and profitability of the Buzzard Academy is enhanced, who will quibble? I think the point has already been made that our academic standing among the tertiary institutions is increasingly moribund, we are the poor cousin to a pair of luxuriating rivals. We cannot gag at trifles. *How* we achieve success in this endeavour will be forgotten quickly enough *if* we achieve success."

2 | Birds of a Feather

"What is that sly falcon up to?"

Dr Plume leaned back on her perch. "The *Journal of Birdology* is a prestigious scientific publication, not an organ for undergraduate pranks."

"It's not a prank Dr Plume. Something more interesting is at work here. Tweet has a yellow spotted kagu in his care—that's been confirmed."

Plume nodded to her colleague. Her bright golden crest rippled with the slightest head movement so that she seemed to be in constant delicate motion. "So why claim to be collaborating in a breeding programme with the Merlin? Where does that assertion get him? It's so easily exposed as a falsehood?"

Professor Swoop shrugged. "Perhaps he really believes we have a specimen?"

Ms Hoopoe, the Merlin Academy bursar, cleared her throat. "Meanwhile, we have received an unprecedented surge in enrolments. Just the mention of our 'acquisition' in this illustrious journal has swollen our coffers."

"Inflated interest in the conservation programmes of the Academy will be short-lived when the truth is revealed," replied Plume.

"And that is problematic to the Academy, Dr Plume. This might seem an artless question addressed to a conclave of academic luminaries, and coming from a *mere* accountant," began Hoopoe, pausing to grind her beak in a subtle dominance display, "but it *is* the elephant bird in the room... why, exactly, don't we have a yellow spotted kagu at our facility?"

"We are talking about an archaic species believed to be long extinct," answered Swoop, stroking her head feathers. "And that's what makes this bird so interesting. You are literally shaking your tail at your evolutionary precursor. We are modern birds, characterised by modern features: aeronautical feathers, functional keeled wings and a sturdy furcula. A primitive bird, by comparison, has a flatter sternum, gastralia in the abdomen—and that's just for starters. Their behaviours and communications would obviously be quite different too. There's literally no limit to what can be learned from studying a living ancestor. You can throw away your textbook and start again."

"Yessss..." nodded Hoopoe. "I believe you were explaining *why* we don't have one of these fascinating animals?"

"Because they are extinct... or they *were* extinct. Which means they're still as rare as hens teeth," quipped Swoop.

"Professor Swoop. If there is one yellow spotted kagu, then it hatched from an egg. Someone, somewhere, laid that egg. Do I need to continue?"

"All that means," retorted Swoop tetchily, "is that there was one other member of this species at the time of the laying."

"Ms Hoopoe makes a salient point Professor," Plume interjected with soothing tones. "As an animal slides toward extinction, there will—of course—be a sole remaining member of that species. But there is a longer arc in any drift to oblivion that includes a breeding pool of these animals. Speculation that Rookery's yellow spotted kagu is the last in his lineage vies with a stronger possibility that a colony of this species still exists in the wild."

The normally somnolent Associate Professor Gentoo chimed in. "I endorse the insightful perspective of Professor Swoop. Why would this kagu fellow have even ventured out unless he were the last of his kind?"

Plume continued smoothly over the interjection. "And if we can arrest that drift toward extinction while this species is still viable, aren't we morally obliged to intercede? Isn't that what our conservation efforts here at the Merlin are about?"

Ms Hoopoe nodded enthusiastically. "Exactly so! And until we have matched our actual resources to the slightly less accurate ones portrayed in the *Journal of Birdology*, it is in the Merlin's reputational—and fiscal—interests to deflect all queries about our juvenile kagu with a bland statement to the effect that we don't want to stress our ward with a media circus."

She pulled a press release from a wing pocket and distributed it around the table.

Swoop shook her head erratically, a distinctive ibis gesture of disbelief. "Are you proposing we make some sort of attempt to locate an actual juvenile of this species?"

"Are you volunteering to lead the expedition, Professor?" Hoopoe replied with a wry smile.

❊ ❊ ❊

Talon furrowed his brow, unconvinced.

"It's the perfect disguise. Let me demonstrate." Chimango placed the leather falcon hood over his head, covering his eyes and framing his beak. It was an elegant embossed hood, a colourful spray of feathers erupting from the top knot, a pair of sleek leather straps issuing from the back.

"There," he said. "There's no chance either of us will be recognised in these stylish disguises."

"Can you see anything at all from inside the hood, Professor?" asked Talon.

"Ah. See your point. Rather dramatic flaw in the plan." He removed the headgear wistfully. "Pity. But we daren't just stroll in there without a disguise. Imagine the scandal if we're recognised!"

"Agreed. What we really need," suggested Talon, "are disguises that point the claw in another direction."

2 | Birds of a Feather

Chimango clicked his beak thoughtfully. "You mean disguises that aren't falcon hoods or eyepatches?"

"Precisely!"

"What have you in mind?"

"We should disguise ourselves in the plumage of another species," Talon said with a casual shrug. "One that is not associated with this institution, but with another."

Chimango's eyes went wide. "That's preposterous! How would that fool anyone? A pair of falcons pretending to be crows or wood pigeons? Ha! We'd be calling attention to ourselves for all the wrong reasons."

"The plan is to break into the compound at night, isn't it?" offered Talon. "I think we'll get away with it in the dark."

"It's the maddest idea I've ever heard," said Chimango, shaking his head. "What sane bird would disguise himself as another species of bird?"

"That is the point Professor, and also why I think it will work." He went to the cabinet behind his desk and pulled out a large white bag that featured a striking 'Earlybird-the-Tailer' emblem.

"What's this?" asked Chimango.

"You recall our visit to the Merlin Academy last fall? That conference on dotterel conservation? The bird of paradise who was department head, what was her name? Plump?"

"Dr Plume I believe. Exotic creature. Smart too for a bird of paradise."

"And her second was an ibis, I don't recall her name... beady eyes, tall and white with a black head... anyway, herewith, one bird of paradise and one white ibis." Talon pulled the ibis plumage from the bag and handed it to Chimango.

"Absurd," remarked Chimango. "This madcap scheme can't possibly work."

"Perhaps... perhaps not..."

Talon excused himself to his antechamber where he slipped out of his falcon plumage and into the bird of paradise. He returned to his office.

Chimango stared in alarm.

"Where is Professor Talon and who, may I ask, are you?"

"Talon," said Talon.

"Yes, the professor. Where has he gone?"

"I'm Talon."

"Professor Talon is a gyrfalcon. You are not a gyrfalcon... some sort of tropical bird of paradise is my guess."

"I'm Talon in disguise. Chimango—I'm Talon!"

"Whoever you are, I fail to see the humour in this prank."

"Excellent."

Talon retired to his antechamber and returned a few moments later in his falcon plumage.

"Ah, Talon, there you are, strangest thing... some showy bird of paradise was just here claiming to be you!"

"Strange indeed."

❄

3 | Midnight in Birdland

A sleek grey-brown saker falcon with an eyepatch stood near the rear entrance scanning the colourful blend of inn patrons. A group of barn owls were engaged in a drinking game at one table. Crows played a raucous game of dice at the next. An elegant heron sat at the bar with a tequila, its live worm writhing in the golden liquid. Three flamingos stood on single legs by the fire sipping pink gins and honking with laughter.

He located a gyrfalcon with an opposing eyepatch seated at one of the corner booths and strolled over with theatrical insouciance.

"Password?" he hissed at the gyrfalcon.

"We only need passwords when we're in full disguise, Professor."

Chimango stood his ground.

Talon sighed. "Death from the skies."

"Good enough." Chimango sat down.

"You located the kagu compound?" asked Talon.

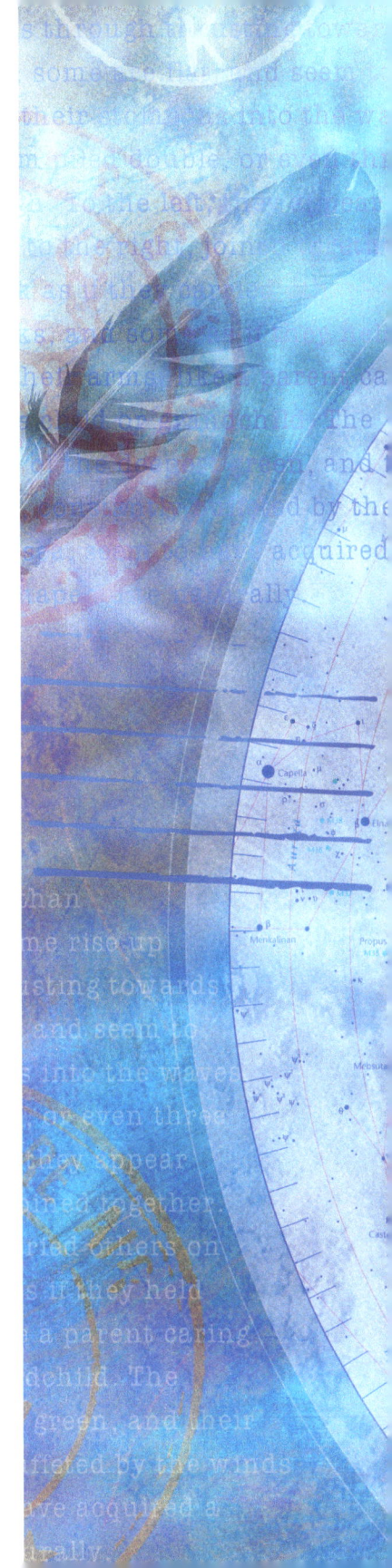

"Better than that. I have a map of the layout and a schedule of guard movements." Chimango pulled a hand-drawn map from his wing pocket and opened it on the table.

"How on earth did you get this?"

"Well... there's a sign at the university, near the main entrance, with all the map details, and a magpie on security there explained the guard movements."

"You asked him and he told you?"

"There was no need to ask. He saw me drawing my map and he came over and offered."

Talon gave a baffled shrug. He studied the sketch of the compound for a couple of minutes.

"We'll need to divert the attention of the duty guard—that's your job, Professor. While he's occupied I'll slip into the compound, unlatch the cage and escort the kagu to our rendezvous point over here," he stabbed at the map with his index talon. "The operation starts at precisely 23.59 hours and we rendezvous at 00.05. Any questions?"

"Divert his attention?"

"Yes. Talk to him. You know, engage him on a topic."

"What do magpies talk about?"

"Sport, mainly, I suppose. Or the weather. Or they complain about their employers. Non-academic university staff constantly gripe about academic staff, in case you haven't noticed. You're an erudite fellow, think of something."

Chimango clicked his beak with a dull expression, then lit up. "I'll go with the weather. I read an interesting research paper on the affects of katabatic wind patterns on albatross navigation—he's bound to find that engaging."

"Good plan. Any more questions?"

"Are you sure the ibis plumage is necessary? These eye patches really do the trick and they look distinguished too."

"We aren't competing for raptorial elegance, Professor. We're laying a trail of breadcrumbs that leads to the Merlin Academy. A bird of paradise and an ibis are seen hanging around the compound before the kagu goes missing. Think about it."

Chimango sighed wistfully. "It's your caper. I just wonder if you're not overthinking the operation is all."

"We'll see. No other questions?"

"The getaway. What's the plan?"

Talon pulled out his map of Upper Birdland, Lower Birdland and the Passerine Peninsula. "We have a full moon tonight. This track," he motioned with a talon, "leads to the beach. We can connect up with another trail around this point. The second track takes us to the Passerine Peninsula. That should give us a healthy start over any pursuers. Then we ask the kagu for our next bearing."

"What happens if we're caught?"

"Hmmmm." Talon glanced at his colleague through a slitted eye. "The best strategy is to tell the truth, old bird. Say you're Professor Chimango from the Buzzard Academy."

"How is that the best strategy? I thought we were trying to lay a false trail?"

"Everyone knows that Professor Chimango is a distinguished saker falcon. An ibis claiming to be a falcon gives a rather suspicious impression that the Merlin Academy is trying to implicate the Buzzard in *their* shenanigans."

Chimango nodded slowly. "You really are a sly fellow aren't you?"

※ ※ ※

Talon hung back and counted off a minute. Long enough for his co-conspirator to have made contact with the guard. He slipped stealthily into the compound and made his way to the caged part of the facility. Curiously the latch to the cage complex was open and the door was even slightly ajar. He hesitated for a moment wondering what that might mean, then he shrugged and went in.

※ ※ ※

To Chimango's astonishment the guard magpie was already engaged in an earnest discussion with a statuesque saker falcon—a dazzling creature with a mostly white head, rich brown wings and slightly tawnier chest speckling than his own.

"You see," said the falcon with an urbane gesture, "a tropical easterly flow, caused by the Coriolis effect, mixes with the valley breeze that normally flows up the slopes of the Raptor Range in summer—which is where I'm from by the way—creating wave turbulence. This turbulence then oscillates..."

She stopped mid-sentence with a look of bewilderment as she caught sight of Chimango stepping out of the shadows. He cut a striking figure in his white ibis plumage—the black wingtips were especially eye-catching and the long curve of his black beak hinted at virility and intelligence.

"Busy enclosure tonight," said Pika, turning to the new arrival. "I suppose you're out for a midnight stroll too?" he asked.

"Ah, yes, quite, that is precisely what I'm doing. Full moon you know," blustered Chimango. He grinned unconvincingly and turned his attention to the falcon. "Forgive me for interrupting... mademoiselle, I don't believe we've met? Did you say Raptor Range?"

"Yes," she spluttered. "No. Yes."

She held out her yellow gloved hand. "Swoop. Alia Swoop."

"I have some acquaintance with the Raptor Range," he said with a cheeky wink. "Chimango. Chuck Chimango." He took her hand and bowed suavely.

She cooed softly with the hint of a giggle. "What a wonderful place this Rookery is. Full of pleasant surprises. Where do you hail from Mr Chimango?"

"Oh please, just Chuck or Chucky. From? Yes, yes... from the Indigo Archipelago... do you know it? I think of Raptor Range as my true home. But one goes where one is needed in the professions and all that."

"Indigo Archipelago? How interesting. I work... um, *studied*... at the Merlin Academy... years ago now, ha ha, not now of course—in my student days, so yes, I'm quite familiar with that province."

"Shall I leave you two to get to know each other?" asked Pica with a sigh.

"Thank you," said Chimango with a dismissive wave.

"The guard and I were just discussing the weather." said Swoop. "The Coriolis effect."

"Ha! I read a fascinating paper recently on the influence of katabatic winds on bird navigation," proffered Chimango.

"Oh! I read an article on that too! In *Aviatrix Today*. Albatross glide on them. How wonderful to meet a scholar on a midnight ramble!

Perhaps you'd care to discuss this invigorating topic at greater depth in warmer surroundings? I have lodgings at an inn not far from here. If the bar is closed we can call on room service for refreshments..."

❄ ❄ ❄

It was dark in the enclosure. Talon saw the hint of a bird silhouette standing in a gloomy corner.

"Don't make a sound," he whispered. "I'm here to rescue you."

"You are?" she replied loudly, with a hint of mirth.

Talon froze. A gyrfalcon stepped into the light. They simultaneously gasped at the appearance of the other. His bird of paradise was even more exotic than her own—a golden tail flecked with luminescent orange and striped bands; a pair of elongated red feathers forming capricious twirls above his head. Her gyrfalcon was snowy white with light grey-brown speckling on the wings, effulgent and delectable. They stared at each other like awkward fledgelings at the school soiree.

"I expected a mottled kagu in these lodgings, not a damsel of surpassing beauty? How is this possible?" inquired Talon.

"I too came to rendezvous with an archaic Eurypygiformes. Sadly I report we are both late, the door to the enclosure was ajar, this flightless bird has flown."

"If each time that destiny deals a miserable buffet to my rear it also sends forth an apparition of spectral radiance, I for one will not quibble with the fates."

"My disappointment with the kagu's elopement is also beginning to subside. I'm Plume, Eurydice Plume."

Talon bowed with a cultivated flourish.

"Oddly I have heard that name before but never associated it with one so comely. I am Talon. As I was the sole hatchling in my brood, no first name was awarded. It is an honour to make your acquaintance, Ms Plume."

"*Miss* Plume, but my friends call me Plume."

"Then I will call you Plume in the hope that I too am admitted into that privileged circle."

Their dalliance was interrupted by the sound of the cage door swinging open with the arrival of a pair of magpies.

Cissa surveyed the scene. "We lose one bird and catch two," he said to Pika.

"Didn't realise the captain was so popular," said Pika.

"*Lose one?*" asked Talon. "You lost the yellow spotted kagu?"

"Escaped a few hours ago," said Cissa with a shrug. "Followed him to the *Marlin*—the boat Lucy left for him to find. He's gone now. If he gets through the reef in the dark, he won't be back. Won't be back if he doesn't either."

"Did you not even try to stop him?"

"My instructions were just to see he didn't get up to any trouble on his dash for the launch."

"Who gave you those instructions? Your employer? Surely not?" Talon said, shaking his head.

"Lucy," said Cissa. "University employs us, but she guides us."

"Lucy? Who is Lucy?" asked Plume.

"A yellow spotted kagu," said Pika. "Unusual for her species, not even remotely argumentative."

"Don't know why she wanted Flegg to escape. He tried to kill her, you know. Tried to torture us too. A very nasty *R. jubatus*," added Cissa.

"Mad as a dodo," said Pika. "Glad to see the back of him."

"Soooo..." said Plume, "there's a second yellow spotted kagu in the area? Out of idle interest, where might we find this Lucy?"

"You won't," said Cissa.

"Unless she wants you to find her," said Pika.

"Magpies!" Talon muttered under his breath.

"Perhaps you could tell us where we might find this Lucy? And in return we might choose not to report these events to your employer. I'm sure Professor Tweet would have something to say about guards enabling his ward to escape," threatened Plume, with no great subtlety.

"What do you think, Pika?" asked Cissa. "Should we lock them up so they can explain to the professors what they were doing in his enclosure when Flegg escaped?"

"How did the kagu escape in the first instance?" responded Pika. "Looks like he had inside help. Perhaps this pair know something?"

"Ha ha, friends, that won't be necessary. My business here is in an unofficial capacity. It was a dark night. I stumbled into this pen looking for a public convenience," said Talon.

"I too am an accidental visitor. Lost my bearings while out moon watching," said Plume. "Don't trouble yourselves, we can find our own way out."

❉ ❉ ❉

There was no sign of either Swoop or Chimango outside the compound. The pair trudged back to the inn where Talon had secured his lodgings. The bar was still being serviced but almost empty. They ordered house wine and some nibbles and retired to a side booth.

"We appear to be pursuing the same objectives, Talon," said Plume. "Perhaps it would be in our mutual interest to align our strategies and share in the spoils?"

"I am more than enthusiastic for the scheme, but I feel compelled by gallantry to make a small confession. I am no common or garden mercenary. I hail from an academy of note—which will remain nameless—where I am a respected faculty member, a prominent professor no less."

"I hereby make the same confession," replied Plume. "It is a wonder to me that our paths have failed to cross in the past? I consider myself to be an aesthete, sensitive to the charms and deficiencies of my peers and would surely remember any such occasion."

"I have an uneasy feeling that our paths have crossed Plume, and yet the notion is nonsensical," murmured Talon. "How could I forget any encounter with such a dazzling creature?"

Snacks and wine goblets were placed on the table by a plump goose.

"It seems we have two choices open to us," said Plume. "One is to pursue the escapee, who is already some distance away on the open sea moving with haste along an unknown trajectory. The other is to locate this Lucy character."

"Let us consider that weighty topic in the morning my dear. I am content for the time being, and for whatever is left of this moonlit night, to compose sonnets dedicated to your extraordinary comeliness."

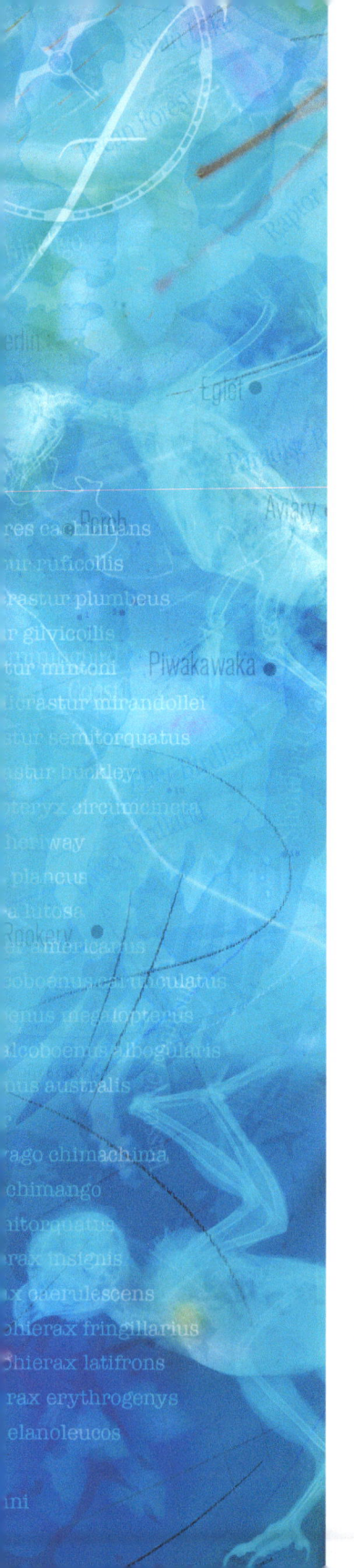

4 | Quest

Talon awoke refreshed despite a long night of acrobatic exertions. Plume had gone in search of breakfast—her lingering presence in the bed chamber distilled to a dent in the mattress.

He considered changing into his falcon plumage as a special treat for her but decided against it until well clear of Rookery. The risk of being identified as an emissary of the Buzzard Academy and linked to the missing kagu had not diminished.

He pondered the evening's escapade beginning with the empty cage and the odd circumstances around the kagu's escape, followed by unexpected revelations of another yellow spotted kagu at large. Then there was the odd disappearance of Chimango. And finally the manifestation of a sultry beauty—as besotted with him as he with her.

Indeed, Plume had shown a remarkable warmth towards his bird of paradise disguise which was both vexing and oddly stimulating. That, at least, delayed any urgency to restore his plumage. She was a rare bird indeed to intuit a fellow falcon so clearly through his obscuring camouflage. He wondered if Chimango was right about these disguises: no one of true substance could be fooled by them.

He bathed, preened, then joined her.

"There's already a buzz around the room, all the conversations are about the missing kagu, Talon," Plume whispered to him conspiratorially. "Birds do like to gossip."

"I confess I'm still dazed by our night's contortions, Dr Eurydice Plume. It will be an hour at least until I have fully regained my senses." He closed his eyes for a few moments to enjoy a memory. "That special innovation of yours—the 'pounce' one—would it work as well without a stack of pillows?"

She giggled coquettishly. "We shall have to trial it and see."

"Consider me your willing accomplice in any and all research projects that capture your imagination, Dr Plume."

"Expect your mettle to be fully tested, Professor Talon," she cooed.

The breakfast arrived, a bowl of mixed cereals, grains and fruit. Talon launched himself at his meal with gusto.

"First priority is to plan our next move on the yellow spotted kagu front. I had an accomplice with me last night, another professor. Presumably she returned to our lodgings having failed in her rather simple assignment of distracting the guard."

"Ha! My accomplice has disappeared entirely, no doubt ashamed to show his face after a similar dismal performance. I was, naturally, not upset to find him missing from our lodgings last night as that meant we had the rooms to ourselves, but now I confess to a small concern at his disappearance. No matter, the substance of our plan remains intact, the quest goes on."

She nodded thoughtfully. "As you say, there is little point in worrying about our companions. More pressing—if there's another yellow spotted in the district, then there is a merchant who will certainly know of her whereabouts."

"Oh?" asked Talon, tilting his head.

"The local tailer. Where else would a yellow spotted obtain a supply of plumage?"

Talon stared at Plume for a few moments. "Your deductions are as uncompromising as your beauty, Miss Plume. Let us dally no longer. I am a bird of action. We will have our kagu by nightfall."

❈ ❈ ❈

"A yellow spotted kagu named Lucy? Ha! I would know if we had one of those on our books. And we do not," said Mr Dickenshaw, Tailer.

"We do cater for a number of endangered species. Not to mention one or two 'unfeasibles'. But there's only one kagu in this district: the Passport Issuing Officer for Upper Birdland, Lower Birdland and the Passerine Peninsula..." said Mrs Dickenshaw.

"And he's an 'ordinary', as we call them in the tailing trade. Standard blue-white. Tall for a kagu, mind you, but not abnormally so," said Mr Dickenshaw, finishing Mrs Dickenshaw's sentence.

"Very officious sort. Argumentative..." she added.

"Weak minded," said Mr Dickenshaw.

"Found himself in the right vocation all right—ordering people around," said Mrs Dickenshaw. "Poor crane that replaced him when he abandoned his post needed new plumage after the scuffle they had when he returned."

"Not my favourite species," said Mr Dickenshaw.

"Not mine either, Mr Dickenshaw," said Mrs Dickenshaw.

"Good customer though," said Mr Dickenshaw. "Always pays his bills promptly."

"Latest technology passports," agreed Mrs Dickenshaw.

❈ ❈ ❈

"Can I help you?" asked the Passport Issuing Officer for Upper Birdland, Lower Birdland and the Passerine Peninsula. He was seated at a desk located on the beach in the dappled shade of a coconut palm.

"We're looking for information," said the rakish bird of paradise.

"Concerning one of your species," added the distinguished falcon.

"A kagu?" Pierrot tilted his head quizzically. "That fellow Flegg who escaped from the university breeding programme? You won't find him. His departure wasn't processed by this office. Left in the dead of night. Most likely met his end on the reef. If he survived that he's on his way back to Falde."

"Falde?" Plume raised an eyebrow quizzically.

"I don't suggest you follow him there. Highly uncivilised place.

Especially dangerous for birds."

"I've never heard of anywhere named Falde? Is it an island beyond the reef?" asked Talon.

"Are there many of his type there?" interjected Plume.

"Like him? Yes. Quite a few," said Pierrot. "We've had most of our tourism from Falde in recent times. Immigrants too. Lucy's from Falde, though she's a Birdlander now. Processed her papers myself. And look, here she is." Pierrot turned his attention to a giggling myna who skidded to a halt beside the desk.

"What are you and Georgie up to?" he enquired.

"Playing hide and seek. Though with Georgie it's mostly hide and sleep," she said laughing.

"He's fond of a nap," she explained in an aside to the visitors.

"You're Lucy?" asked Plume with surprise, staring down at Lucy.

"Lucy, Myna, Yellow Spotted," said Lucy, drawing attention to her dashing plumage. "Pleased to meet you. Georgie would say hello too but he's hiding in the bushes." She waved in a vague direction along the treeline.

Plume gave Talon a sideways look.

"You don't, by any outside chance, know a pair of magpies do you Lucy, Myna, Yellow Spotted?" asked Talon.

"Cissa and Pica are my friends," replied Lucy. "They came to my party. I'm nine," she proudly announced.

"Hmmm," said Plume.

"Lucy bosses that pair around quite a bit," said Pierrot with a chuckle. "But you know magpies... following orders is in their nature. In the breeding, you might say."

"We spoke to that pair last night as a matter of fact. They mentioned Lucy," said Plume.

"Well, who can resist talking about a yellow spotted myna? But I'd guess they were probably talking about another Lucy." He sighed wistfully.

"Another Lucy... a kagu?" asked Plume, perking up.

"A very special kagu. She was here just a few hours ago." He pulled a feather cloth from his wing pocket, took off his glasses and cleaned them.

"Where is she now?" asked Talon. "We'd like to talk to her."

"Gone," he said, gesturing towards the sea.

"She didn't say where she was going?" asked Plume.

"I don't think she knows herself," he shrugged. "If you find her, say hello from me... ah look behind you, it's our mutual friends!"

Cissa and Pika emerged from the treeline on the track to Rookery. They stopped to greet Lucy who skipped along the beach to intercept them. An animated discussion broke out on the topic of hide and seek tactics. Lucy scampered off to continue her game and the magpies joined the group around Pierrot's desk.

"We're supposed to arrest you two," said Pika to the falcon and the bird of paradise, "as suspects in the case of the missing kagu."

"But we won't," said Cissa. "It had nothing to do with either of you, despite your best efforts to incriminate yourselves."

"Would be smart to disappear. We aren't the only magpies with orders to apprehend the suspicious strangers seen lurking around the kagu enclosure last night," added Pica.

"Oh! These two were there when Flegg escaped?" Pierrot said to the magpies. He turned back to his colourful visitors. "I suppose that explains why you want to talk to Lucy. You have an interest of some sort in yellow spotted kagus, I take it?"

"A purely academic one," improvised Plume. "We're engaged in a research project to do with endangered species. A living archaic variant of an already rare species is quite a big deal in our field. As a kagu yourself you must have an inkling how important sightings of a yellow spotted are to those of us working in the conservation field."

Talon nodded in agreement.

"Midnight researchers," said Pica with a wink.

"Stealthy methodologies," added Cissa.

"Our methodologies are necessarily obtuse to the lay-bird. Paleotaxonomic conservation research is a complex field," said Talon defensively.

"Nonetheless, we'll collect our luggage from Rookery immediately and make haste with our departure. I don't want to be caught up in any local university politics," said Plume, adjusting her beak.

"Your personal effects are at the magpie station," said Cissa. "You'll be arrested if you go back to Rookery."

"My plumage!" cried Talon.

"Damn," muttered Plume.

"But if you want to avoid that you can take the coastal track north from here, it bypasses Rookery and winds through the jungle to Gull. Ferries link to Aves from there," said Pika, "our jurisdiction ends on the Birdland border."

"I can find you a few supplies for your journey, if that's helpful" said Pierrot.

"And we'll guide you to the track," offered Cissa.

❈ ❈ ❈

"Lagoon ferry leaves in 10 minutes, Talon. The Rookery to Aviary ferry is coming in now. It departs in 15 minutes. If we catch that one we'll be in Merlin before sunset."

"I'm inclined to dawdle," Talon pursed his beak. "Lagoon ferry, let's take the scenic route home. We're empty-handed. There's the small matter of one's pride to consider my dear. The name *Talon* is not interchangeable with *failure*."

"Failure? We were sabotaged by a cruel twist of fate—that damned kagu spoiled his rescue by escaping first! And it's rather too obvious that we were let down by our accomplices," she consoled.

Talon scratched his chin. "The ignominy of being harangued out of rookery like a common thief sticks disagreeably in my craw. Even so I would consider a prompt return to my eyrie at the academy but for one crucial detail. I am travelling in the company of Dr Eurydice Plume. The more time we spend together rambling through meadows, pausing by this charming nook or that romantic cranny, at star-rise marching in triumph to the bed chamber—the less urgent the sting of a thwarted mission will seem."

"Lagoon ferry it is," she cooed in agreement.

❈ ❈ ❈

Plume and Talon took perches near the middle of the ferry. When all the passengers were seated a swan hostess addressed them.

"Attention birds of prey, shorebirds, seabirds, migrants and wanderers. The Captain has turned on the Fasten Perch Belt sign.

If you haven't already done so, please stow your carry-on luggage underneath the perch in front of you or in the central bin. Make sure your perch-back and feeding trays are in their full upright position.

"If you are seated in waddle class, please remember to peddle. This craft works best when all passengers peddle in unison. We remind you that this is a non-squawking service. Squawking is prohibited on the entire craft, including the lavatories. If you have any questions about our sailing today, please don't hesitate to ask one of our waterfowl. Thank you."

The announcement was followed by a safety pantomime performed by cabin crew in the central aisle of the vessel which amounted to climbing overboard, floating and honking in the case of an emergency.

The ferry pulled away from Gull Quay, pirouetted, and slid out of the harbour in a stately fashion. Just beyond Gull Head, it veered into Birdland Strait, a picturesque channel separating Birdland to the south from Aves—the largest and most populous of the islands in the Chimes group—to the north.

The coastline of Birdland was unmistakably tropical, its coral reef outcrops and white sand beaches fringing a coconut palm jungle that stretched back to low verdant hills covered in banana trees, kapok and jackfruit.

Aves presented a more tortured volcanic coastline dotted with mangroves, its rugged interior quilted in rainforests and scrublands. A high range arched like an extruded spine that cut though the island—forested foothills clambering toward daunting peaks, their white tips concealing an impenetrable, and unexplored, terrain on its eastern flanks. Clouds hung like gossamer scarves around the highest of the peaks, lending them a brooding atmosphere

❆ ❆ ❆

Lagoon was a colourful port town, its waterfront bustling with markets, warehouses and stalls. Two streets back from the waterfront, Talon and Plume found comfortable lodgings at the Shining Cuckoo, an iconic wayfarer's retreat just a stone's throw from the old town square.

Gulp the innkeeper, a portly pelican, looked them up and down with a beady gaze. "You only want one room?" he queried with a scowl. "We have double beds in each of our rooms, but only one per room."

"One will do nicely," said Talon brightly.

"Falcons and tropical birds nesting together?" Gulp raised an eyebrow. "Is this one of those new big city fashions?"

Talon chuckled. "Don't be deceived by appearances, good sir. The doctor and I have a lot more in common than you might imagine."

Plume chirped in agreement.

The innkeeper shook his head bemused. "What patron's get up to in their rooms is no business of mine," he said, "so long as they keep the squawking down. Other guests are here to get a good night's rest."

"We're academics on what has been a fruitless quest to locate an animal sighted in Birdland believed to be long extinct—a yellow spotted kagu," said Plume to change the topic of conversation.

"Dime a dozen in these parts," quipped Gulp.

"What?" demanded Talon.

"One here last night. On her way up the coast she was."

"Surely you're mistaken!"

"Not at all. No mistaking a kagu. Odd birds. Not usually my cup of tea as a species, but this one was nice enough."

"A yellow spotted? Was her name Lucy?" pressed Talon.

"Aye. And she wasn't remotely argumentative either. Very un-kagu-like," Gulp said, stroking his throat pouch, the way pelicans do.

"On her way up which coast?" asked Plume.

"East I suppose," he said, shrugging. "Seemed to be aimlessly exploring the islands. Nice occupation for some... she took one of our maps and asked a few questions about the Shorebird Coast. Took some provisions."

❊ ❊ ❊

"I say we take the coastal road. It's longer, but she could be anywhere between here and Gannet. There are small villages dotted along the coastline," Plume traced the coast with her index talon along their map. "Gannet township is at the end of the road. It's the end of civilisation too. Just north of there the Soaring Range forms an impassable barrier. There are no boat landings on the other side of the range until you navigate around the whole spur and into Wader Inlet.

N
NW
NE
W
E
SW
SE
S
The Chimes
Puffin Bay
Raven Wilds
Aviary
AVES
Eglet
Swan Lake
Stork Inlet
Raptor Range
Condor
Owlet
Indigo Archipelago
Merlin
Wader Inlet
Soaring Range
Nuna Wilds
Albatross Cliffs
Perch
ADZE
Razor Rocks
Gannet
Gannet Rocks
Hummingbird Coast
Lagoon
Gull
Upper Birdland
Shorebird Coast
Lower Birdland
Rookery
BIRDLAND
Passerine Peninsula

The Razor Rocks bar your passage through that channel. And Nuna Wilds terminate in a series of sheer cliffs anyway. Adze Island is even worse. There's a reason that side of the mountains is uninhabited."

Plume paused and looked at Talon. "So once she gets to Gannet she can only sail back the way she came. Hopefully we'll intercept her going up the coast or coming back."

Talon nodded slowly. He sipped his water. "What's the plan when we find her? She doesn't need rescuing, is unlikely to want to be studied, and may not want to point us to her homelands."

"If she agrees to accompany us back to our respective institutions we can get a lot of mileage from exhibiting her and doing an informal study of the species. And if she doesn't, you and I might co-author a book about our experiences... *Back from the Brink—The Search for the Lost Kagu*, or *Lucy—The Living Fossil*. We can come out of this with academic credits either way."

"Where have you been all my life, Dr Plume?" he shook his head admiringly.

❄ ❄ ❄

The Old Coastal Highway was little more than a penguin track snaking its way around the Shorebird Coast. After a day's hike, the pair found lodgings at the Albatross Inn in Lower Cormorant, a small fishing village tucked in behind Oystercatcher Spit.

A bank of black clouds rolled in from the sea, bringing a storm that lasted two days and trapped them in their room. To wile away the time, Plume instigated a curriculum of amorous experiments. Her latest programme was brimming with artistic contortions—a number of them especially challenging—testing suppleness, flexibility and endurance. Talon, more than equal to the rigorous demands, added his own eccentric flourishes and side entertainments.

They emerged from their love-nest on the third morning, into a thick sea fog that blanketed the coast. An hour along the trail the low clouds burned away, revealing a long flat pebbled beach that disappeared into haze in both directions. All signs of the Old Coastal Highway had melted into sand, shells, driftwood and seaweed.

Their coastal trek was uneventful and by late afternoon they were comfortably ensconced at the bar of the Blind Gannet, a haunt of local fisherbirds. Talon fell into conversation with a pair of boobies at the bar—a species renowned for their interest in gossip—to ask if anyone had sighted a yellow spotted kagu or might know her whereabouts. He was directed to an albatross wearing an eyepatch sitting alone in the corner.

"Aye," said the albatross, a boat's captain named Screech. "She was sitting last night where you're sitting now. What's your interest in her?"

"We're academics," began Plume.

"The yellow spotted kagu has been extinct for tens of thousands of years," said Talon.

"Except that, as it turns out, they're not extinct, and that has dramatic implications for the field of ornithology," continued Plume.

"She's the taxonomic discovery of the century," agreed Talon.

"We're interested in the rescue and conservation of her species. We want to interview her about her origins, determine the viability of the breeding pool, assist in its recovery," said Plume.

"And because she's an archaic species, we can learn a lot about our own evolutionary history from her," added Talon.

Screech nodded. "And what if she doesn't want your assistance?" he asked.

"We're not planning to chicknap her," said Talon.

"We're reputable professors, not gangsters," added Plume, nodding vigorously.

"This isn't a university town, it's a fishing town... hub of the Aves fishing industry. We don't get *flashy* birds in these parts." He stared pointedly at Talon who stood out rather starkly with his iridescent colouring and shimmering feather extensions amid the mainly black and white seabird patrons of the inn.

Talon shuffled uncomfortably on his perch. "That's as may be Captain Screech. One cannot alter one's plumage. We are what we are. Can you assist us to find Lucy?" he asked.

He held Talon's gaze and nodded slowly. "She questioned me about the state of the coastline north of here with the last storm, out beyond Plover Point. There's nowhere to land a vessel on the Nuna Coast, apart from a small cove and a sea cave, accessed by a narrow passage this side of the Razors, just on the other side of the range. Fishing boats use it as shelter when they're caught out and the weather turns. Shelter Cave has a small jetty and a hut that was built there for fishers to wait out storms."

Plume pulled out her map for guidance and Captain Screech indicated the position of the cave.

"The odd thing," he continued, "is that the hut is always well supplied. Fresh food and fuel for the fire. Locals say there's a bird spirit on that side of the range who looks out for mariners. No one's ever seen it, of course."

"And you think Lucy went there?"

"Aye," said the albatross. "That's where she went."

5 | Nuna

Wispy mist rolled on the water around fishing boats and under gantries and piers. Gannet Marina was home to a colourful array of trawlers, long liners and other paddle craft that oscillated between moorings. At first light the port swarmed with activity: crews checking nets and lines; loading berley and supplies; assembling for roster on their craft.

Captain Screech waited on Pier 3 beside the *Kingfisher*. All around him fishing boats slipped loose from their berths, stirring the mist as they paddled out past the breakwater, fixing their courses and heading off to favoured fishing grounds.

Having accepted the commission to ferry Plume and Talon to Shelter Cave, Screech had assembled a crew, two burly emperor penguins were installed at their paddle stations, awaiting his command.

The professors—subdued and dishevelled from another night's callisthenics—ambled onto the pier.

"Ahoy captain," said Talon, doing his best to sound salty. "Ahoy mateys," he waved to the penguins. They ignored his greeting and continued their phlegmatic conversation.

"Emperors don't take to fancy city birds," Screech informed him by way of explanation as he guided the pair to perches in the wheelhouse.

The sea looked dark and unsettled. A bank of blue-black cumulus solidified the horizon, blending into random patches of hazy squall on the sea. The smell of brine and ozone hung heavily in the air.

"Another storm's coming. Might be a few days before we can get back to collect you... we don't like the Razors in bad weather," said the captain.

Talon nodded. "We have supplies to last a week," he confirmed. "But we're just as likely to return with you on this voyage if Lucy is easy to locate and amenable to our proposal."

Two hours from port the *Kingfisher* rounded Plover Point where the coastal currents churned together and the sea surface danced. They slid into a narrow channel framed by steep white cliffs on the landward side and dangerous looking rocks to starboard. The Razors were named for their appearance, calcified skeletal remains—a giant metropolis of marine invertebrates—that erupted as pinnacles from the sea floor. As the spires breached the surface they resembled bony fingers pointing accusingly at the sky.

Captain Screech gave them a wide berth. "It's the ones you don't see, the ones just under the surface..."

They turned into Shipwreck Cove and passed beneath a pair of rock arches, then jagged back into a large cave. A small white sailboat, the *Luciana*, bobbed freely on the water, not tied up or anchored. Screech gave the boat a long look and shrugged.

"That's her yacht," he said as much to himself as to his passengers.

He tied the *Kingfisher* to the jetty and assisted Talon and Plume to disembark. The professors stretched their legs. Smoke was coiling lazily from the hut's chimney. They sauntered to the door, gave one another a knowing look, knocked and went in.

A few moments later they came back out. Screech tilted his head.

"Gone," said Talon. "Fire's still glowing—she must be nearby."

"You'll be needing your supplies," said the captain, placing Talon's knapsack on the jetty. "If the weather's over quickly, we'll be back in three days."

He unhooked the boat from the jetty, took the wheel and nodded at the penguins. The *Kingfisher* turned in a wide arc and exited the cave.

❋ ❋ ❋

The professors wasted no time exploring the rock shelter. The hut and jetty were mounted on a wide ledge projecting from the cave wall. It narrowed near the back of the chamber where the walls tapered and led into a tunnel, winding away into semi-darkness. A modest amount of illumination came from a series of vents high above as the passage followed a narrow stream for a distance to its spring, a bubbling pool in a cul de sac.

The pair searched the small gloomy chamber for any sort of branching tunnel or egress but none was evident.

As they retraced their steps from the pool Plume felt a subtle breeze on her face. She looked for its source. The roots of a tree hung down one wall in a filamented curtain that she pushed aside to reveal a narrow passage.

She motioned to Talon and the pair squeezed through, finding themselves in a larger chamber—a wide chimney that was open to the sky. They climbed a rough hewn staircase spiraling around the sides and eventually found themselves on a plateau above the cliff. From there a well used walking track snaked inland.

The rain clouds were closer now, accompanied by an icy chill.

"We could wait it out in the hut," suggested Talon, staring at the approaching weather system.

"Storm could take a while to pass through," said Plume. "We're hot on her tail. Let's push on."

He nodded in agreement and the pair set off along the track. It threaded up a steep incline to a broader plateau then plunged into dense bush. As they made their way beneath a low canopy of tree palms, tea trees and seed ferns the first large raindrops began to splatter around them.

Thereafter the sky thundered and released its deluge. The bush danced to the rain's hammering, affording no shelter. Wet, cold and miserable they trudged on. A distance along the track the bush gave way to a forest of giant conifers, fern trees, ginkgos and cycads.

A faint scent of sulphur hung in the wet air. Steam erupted randomly from hissing vents scattered around the rock strewn forest floor. A small brook, overhung with ferns, meandered alongside the track, its passage broken by mossy rocks and swirling pools. The scene was a mixture of ancient flora and earthy smells. The effect was prehistoric—eerie and evocative.

The track eventually opened up into a large clearing. To their astonishment a cluster of dwellings sat at the centre.

"Birds!" declared Plume, shaking her head.

"I don't believe it," echoed Talon, equally astounded.

They walked into the small village. It consisted of a number of residences in concentric rings around a small cobbled plaza. The dwellings were clearly inhabited with smoke issuing from chimneys, but no one could be seen.

"Where are they?" Talon wondered aloud.

Plume turned to look down a wide track. Faint voices were discernible. They followed the sounds and came to a terraced lake, its uppermost level fuelled by a searingly hot spring that cascaded down twenty-something silicate encrusted levels—each level becoming progressively cooler as the water descended—finally spilling lukewarm into a broad pool at the base.

At least fifty birds sat in pools on middle and lower terraces. The highest levels, sizzling and steaming, were clearly too hot for bathing. Among the clusters of birds were family groups in high spirits, friends and couples sitting together chattering, blissfully warmed, unconcerned about the rain.

"So many emus?" Talon whispered to Plume.

"Odd looking emus, I don't recognise this subspecies," she whispered back.

Not far away, alone in one of the warmer pools, a banded kestrel waved them over, indicating for them to join her. They did and immediately relaxed. The water was at a delicious temperature. Plume cooed with delight.

"You're not from around these parts," noted the kestrel.

"Indeed we are not," replied Talon. "We weren't even aware this region is inhabited! How is this possible?"

"Are you from Aves? Or Birdland?" she enquired.

"We're both from Aves," said Talon, "although we've travelled directly from Birdland on this trip. We were following a kagu, a yellow spotted. She must have passed this village not long ago. Did you see her?"

The kestrel nodded. "She came through this morning. Heading north. She'll be in Pteryx by now, I imagine."

"Pteryx?" asked Talon.

"Main town in these parts. You're in the village of Roc. You're sitting in the Roc Pools," she said, indicating the terraces. "So why are you pursuing this yellow spotted kagu?"

"Ah," replied Plume. "We're ornithologists, from two universities north and northeast of here. Yellow spotted kagus have been extinct for millennia. It's quite a big thing that one or two of them are still extant."

"We want to talk to the kagu," continued Talon. "Find out how it's possible her species has survived to the present. Do a scientific study of them."

"A scientific study?" asked the kestrel. "Do you mean a *display her skeleton at the academy* kind of study?"

"Oh no," answered Plume. "My academy is interested in conservation, not preservation. We just want information and to extend help if it's needed."

The kestrel nodded slowly.

"So how is it you know about Birdland and Aves but we haven't heard of anyone living on this side of Soaring Range?" asked Plume.

"Perhaps the academies on this side of the range are better informed?" offered the kestrel with a wink. "Roc is a spa village. These cascading terraces are the main attraction here. You'll find comfortable accommodation at the Spa Inn on the far side of the lake—that's where I'm staying. I don't recommend continuing on to Pteryx in this weather with evening nearly upon us."

"I'm frankly amazed there are so many birds here," said Talon, looking around the pools. "If you birds know the geography west of the Soaring Range, there must have been some crossover between our communities?"

The falcon shrugged. "Shall we remove to the inn to discuss the matter? You look like you might enjoy an opportunity to freshen up and perhaps sample the local cuisine. Roc ales are excellent."

❆ ❆ ❆

Dry, warm and replete on a meal of sauteed molluscs, seed bread and spiced sausages washed down with a flask of guava wine, Talon perched on a comfortable padded sofa by a roaring fire to converse with the kestrel. Plume had taken her leave briefly to record the day's adventure in her field diary.

"What's a beautiful banded kestrel doing in a village of ratites on the wrong side of the Range?" asked Talon flirtatiously, emboldened by his second flask of wine.

The kestrel gave Talon an appraising look. "It's uncommon—in my experience—for birds to comment on the comeliness of birds of another feather." She raised an eyebrow inquisitively.

"A small confession," said Talon. "You and I are closely related species. You may also have noticed that Dr Plume and I are warm toward one another. This will likely shock you but the reason is straightforward. For various reasons I find myself wearing the plumage of a bird of paradise. I am a gyrfalcon, anxious to reinstate my correct plumage at the first possible convenience. Is there is a good tailer in Pteryx by any chance?"

The kestrel was nonplussed by his revelation. "There's a fine tailor in Pteryx but alas, she doesn't carry gyrfalcon on her racks. So... you have informed Dr Plume of this irregularity and she has no issue with your plumage?"

"Dr Plume is remarkable. She knew from our first meeting that I am a falcon. The topic has never required elaboration."

"I see," nodded the kestrel. "Would it be indelicate to inquire why you're wearing eccentric plumage?"

"Delicate is the word, yes." He leaned forward and lowered his voice, "I was engaged in a legitimate rescue attempt which nevertheless may have reflected badly on the Buzzard Academy. I'm a senior lecturer there, you see. This disguise was an unconventional way of masking my link with the Academy."

"A rescue?"

"The University of Rookery was holding a yellow spotted kagu, a male, in captivity for some pie-in-the-sky breeding programme, presumably against the fellow's will. At any rate he escaped before I could rescue him—well, before *we* could rescue him, that's where I met Dr Plume. She was engaged in her own rescue attempt. We met in his empty cage."

"I see," said the kestrel. "And Dr Plume is from another academy?"

"The Merlin," he nodded.

"Why, out of the myriad choices available, did you choose a bird of paradise for your disguise?" she probed.

"That is a particularly delicate matter," he said, shuffling uncomfortably. "You won't say a word to my colleague?"

"My beak is sealed."

"The Merlin by an odd coincidence has another Professor Plume on its staff who is a bird of paradise. I thought a similar plumage to that one might muddy the waters somewhat, especially if I was seen or apprehended at Rookery... a false trail, etcetera."

"I can see why you don't want that sleight-of-claw broadcast. Very cunning, Professor. Sorry we haven't yet exchanged names?"

"Talon. Professor Talon. But please just call me Talon."

The kestrel held out her yellow gloved hand. "I am Luciwa Peregrine."

Talon clasped it and executed a seated bow.

"I see Dr Plume is about to rejoin us." She nodded to the approaching falcon. "I have a story to share with you both, and a modest proposal."

Plume took a perch beside Talon, initiating polite greetings and small talk.

Drinks were served by a medium sized ratite, a glass of water for Lucy and a myrtle honey wine for Plume.

When they were settled, Lucy began. "I think you two may find there are more exciting fish to fry than that yellow spotted kagu you're chasing."

Plume furrowed her brow. "It's hard to imagine anything more exciting than rediscovering an extinct species, certainly from an ornithological perspective."

"I agree Dr Plume," said Lucy. "And on that point I have a question for you both. Do the emus in this town look odd to you at all?"

"I was about to raise the subject with you," said Plume. "I'm sorry, you have me at a disadvantage. You know my name—you are?"

"Luciwa Peregrine. I'm a paleornithologist. I was attached to the University of Rookery but now I'm doing independent field research."

"Oh, you're not a local. That explains how you know about Birdland and Aves!" exclaimed Talon.

Lucy nodded. "These emus," she continued, "are not emus. They are moa."

She paused to allow that to sink in. They both stared at her.

"Note the differences between them in size and feather speckling. The one who served us is a heavy-footed moa. The big one who led you to your room, a giant moa, *Dinorsis robustus*. I have so far catalogued all nine species of extinct moa. All are alive and well right here in Roc.

"In Pteryx you will find extinct huia, adzebill, dodo, great auk, Haast's eagles. You have stumbled into a *lost world* Professors, where the clock has rewound, or perhaps never moved forward. I stumbled into it myself quite by accident several years ago."

Plume turned to stare at the waitress who was serving another table, then at the customers. "How could we have missed it, Talon? There are two bush moa at the next table and a crested moa behind the bar!"

"This is outlandish. Impossible even," said Talon, aghast.

"And yet, here we are surrounded by species that were thought to have perished hundreds and even thousands of years ago. In Pteryx I encountered a mihirung, supposedly extinct for tens of thousands of years."

Plume called the waitress over. "Excuse me," she asked. "Are you a moa?"

The waitress giggled. "Of course."

"Remarkable," muttered Talon as she shuffled off.

"If you discovered these birds several years ago, Ms Peregrine, why did you not publish this information. It's the single greatest discovery in the history of ornithology, the implications are deeply profound," demanded Plume.

"Yes," said Lucy. "So let me explain. These birds are not endangered. My rough estimate is that a sixth of the entire population of birds living in Aves, live right here on the Nuna Plateau. There are two big towns on this side of the range and numerous villages.

"These birds are not unhappy either. You witnessed them splashing in the terraces and enjoying themselves. What happens if we announce this lost world on the western side of the range? Colonisation? Tourism?"

Talon and Plume stared at Lucy. She continued.

"Right now they are living in their natural habitat. There is no better place or time to study them without interfering with them. To capture their social structure, their customs, their culture. Tell the world they are here and this once-only opportunity is lost forever. If their world merges with the modern world we gain nothing and lose everything. Think about it?"

Plume slowly nodded. Talon said, "you mentioned a proposal?"

"I did," replied Lucy. "It's a simple one. You two are respected ornithologists. And you are here at the historical nexus, a rewriting of bird history. Message your respective academies—I can courier the dispatch for you—that you have made a momentous discovery, the find of the millennium, but that you cannot reveal its location. Others will swoop if you do. Rival institutions will want a slice of the discovery and create pandemonium. Say you will immediately relocate to the field to study these animals in depth, in their natural habitat.

"And do just that. Make a thorough study. Publish your findings as you go to keep your academies happy. Write books on the topic as world authorities, but keep the location secret. You could even infer that you have travelled out beyond the reef to do this research so that no one guesses you are here on Aves, just a stone's throw away."

"What of you?" asked Plume. "This was your discovery?"

"Well, it's up to you," said Lucy. "If you're not keen on pursuing this I have material already prepared for publication under my name, which may not, in the final analysis, be as insightful as your own observations, but it would certainly link me to this discovery in perpetuity. However, you are my academic seniors. Your analysis will have a rigor and gravitas mine lacks. I'm content to hand the discovery and management of this to those better equipped and connected in the field, for the betterment of science."

Talon nodded.

"Of course," Lucy added pensively, "this puts the pair of you in very close proximity to one another for the foreseeable future. There are no other gyrfalcons or birds of paradise in Nuna. You would be engaged in a cause greater than your individual comfort. It is a sacrifice that would be hard for anyone to make on a personal level, and particularly hard when you are the only local examples of your species."

"Oh, we'll do just fine," said Plume with a cryptic smile. She tousled Talon's head feathers affectionately.

"There is one more point to consider," said Lucy. "The mihirung I spoke to claimed to have travelled from Adze and suggested there was an even more ancient cluster of believed-to-be-extinct birds on that island, including *Titanis!* The discovery of recently extinct species on the Nuna plateau may be a portal to something bigger and more primordial than anyone can imagine."

6 | Plumage II

I have an exciting surprise for you Miss Alia Swoop. Meet me for breakfast at the Hen and Chickens' Cafe, 9 sharp.
Chup-tuk!
—Chuck C.

There was no sign of Talon at the inn but his bed had been slept in. Given the details of their escape plan, that implied the kagu rescue attempt may have failed. Chimango decided it could wait, he'd locate Talon and discuss the mission later. Far more pressing was a looming breakfast date with the delectable Professor Swoop.

He discarded his ibis disguise, changing back into his elegant saker falcon plumage and made haste to their assignation.

The night spent in her nest had been one of intimate courtship and ardent mating ritual—circling around her as she reclined, performing high-speed aerobatics while deploying his special "chup-tuk" mating call. Swoop had clearly been dazzled by Chimango's erotic system.

She said repeatedly that his eccentric

flourishes and innovations transcended what might be expected from even the most experimental "ibis" (such a clever joke). Her own manifestations and amorous embraces were exotic to say the least—unusual, delightful, persuasive and impulsive.

And she had not been fooled by his silly ibis disguise, of course, despite the dark hour and Talon's contrary assertion. Nonetheless, if she had any qualms at all about Chuck Chimango as breeding material, he was confident that his morning's plumage transformation would seal the deal.

Chimango arrived at the cafe but there were no falcons to be seen. He was a few minutes late and fretted that he might have missed her. A tall, awkward, somewhat sterile looking white ibis sat alone at a table watching the door. He perched at the next table and, catching her beady eye, asked if perchance she'd seen a statuesque saker falcon in the cafe.

"No," she said. "No one remotely fitting that description. But I've only been here 15 minutes."

There was something curious about her voice and the way she tilted her head when she spoke that reminded him of someone else, but the context eluded him completely.

"I'm sorry, have we met somewhere? You look vaguely familiar to me?"

"I have the same sense about you, but can't imagine where we've met. I am Professor Swoop of the Merlin Academy."

"Ha!" declared Chimango. "I know another Professor Swoop. In fact she is the very falcon I'm meant to be meeting here. And, as a matter of coincidence, you and I met once, albeit rather briefly—at a conference on dotterels last fall. I'm Professor Chimango from the Buzzard."

"Chimango?" she said, surprised. "An unexpectedly common name from that region! What brings another professor from the Raptor Range to Rookery?"

"I have an interest in archaic kagus. I'm an ornithologist."

She nodded. "Same."

A pair of magpies entered the cafe, looked around and settled their gazes on the professors. They walked over to the seated birds.

"We're looking for a gyrfalcon and a bird of paradise," said one.

"Suspicious pair. Decidedly shady," said the other.

"Perhaps you've seen them," said the first, "you two being out-of-towners?"

"I have no knowledge of the bird pairing that you describe," replied Chimango haughtily.

"Nor I," said Swoop with a dismissive gesture. "Such an unusual pair would not have escaped my notice—I pride myself on an acute observational faculty. Just what is your interest in these birds, gentlemen?"

"Our yellow spotted kagu escaped from his compound last night. Dangerous bird. Unpleasant, even by kagu standards."

"Total psychopath if you ask me," echoed the other magpie. "A gyrfalcon and a bird of paradise were in his enclosure around midnight. We have some questions for them."

"They can help us with our investigation," said the first.

Chimango shrugged his shoulders. "I'm sorry, I'm ignorant of these matters and cannot assist you in your quest, officers."

The magpies nodded and looked around the cafe, then departed.

"Oh!" exclaimed Chimango, rubbing his talons together. "So the kagu escaped. The plan worked."

"You know about the rescue plan?" Swoop looked at him shocked.

Chimango looked back at her in alarm. "You know about this too?"

"I don't know who the gyrfalcon was, but I suspect the bird of paradise they're seeking was none other than my esteemed colleague, Dr Plume."

"The gyrfalcon was almost certainly Professor Talon..." he trailed off and stared at her. "Wait... were there two kagu rescue attempts last night?"

Swoop gave Chimango a long penetrating look. "And only one rescue. That explains why Dr Plume didn't return to our lodgings last night. She has the kagu. Ha! Our plan was successful... and I presume that means yours failed. Bad luck, Professor."

Chimango considered Talon's used bed. "Damn," he said, thumping the table. "It's downright greedy of you spiriting the kagu away when you already have one at your academy!"

Swoop winked and tapped her beak.

Chimango studied the ibis, a species he found unpleasant at the best of times. This one seemed particularly ungainly and mean spirited. "The thought occurs to me that those two magpies will be interested in the details of your colleague's 'rescue'. Perhaps I should call them back?"

"And implicate yourself in a failed attempt?"

"What can you prove on that score? And if you do indeed have the kagu," quipped Chimango, "your trustworthiness when it comes to pointing the claw at others is murky at best. Far more likely is that Professor Talon learned of the Merlin plot and was trying to intercept this heinous act on behalf of Rookery University. He is, after all, a high-minded gyrfalcon and a scholar."

"Bah!" said Swoop. "You wouldn't dare."

"The magpies are just across the road. Stay here while I fetch them."

"Wait! Let's not be hasty. Perhaps we can negotiate." She rearranged herself uncomfortably on her perch. "What is it that you want?"

Chimango smiled broadly. "We both want the kagu. Some sort of bird-sharing arrangement might be beneficial to our mutual academies."

She stared at him with an unpleasant expression, the sort you might produce when the insect you're snacking on turns out to be a stink beetle.

"Hence the saying: *sit a falcon on your scat, not your eggs.*"

"You are rather crass aren't you Professor Swoop? It is a huge relief to me that your namesake is cut from an altogether more charming feathercloth."

"I know a more agreeable Professor Chimango too, for what it's worth," she sneered.

Chimango, ignored her peevish insult. "We must locate your confederate along with the kagu."

Swoop stared at him a while longer and sighed. "So be it." She pulled a map from her wing pocket and opened it out. "We had a rendezvous point here," she stabbed a nail at the map, a beach at the intersection of Lower Birdland and the Passerine Peninsula.

"Let us head there now to formalise our new contract."

❈ ❈ ❈

The falcon and the ibis stood on the beach staring at grooves in the sand made by a departed launch and a pile of soggy crumpled plumage. It was yellow with white spots. Swoop turned away and shook her head.

"What happened here?" asked Chimango, perplexed.

"Who knows? All we can say for certain is that this particular kagu is now extinct. Let us hope he was not the last of his species."

Chimango stooped down and picked up the plumage. He folded it up carefully and placed it in his shoulder bag.

"Wait a moment," said Swoop, holding out a wing. "That plumage is the property of the Merlin Academy. Pass it to me at once."

Chimango surveyed her with a serene countenance. "I can find no trace of irony in your demand, and yet it is without a fleck of authority."

"We have a pact to share the spoils in this enterprise," she protested.

"I believe our agreement was to share in the custodianship of the yellow spotted kagu. Nothing regarding his plumage or any other portion of his bodily remains was discussed."

"Your reputation for grotesque humour grows by the instant, Professor Chimango. The spoils of our venture are not a valid topic for renegotiation—these actions amount to a semantic parlour trick. I demand a reconsideration of your buffoonish stance."

"There may be some merit in this protest, despite your rather petulant and disagreeable insults, though I fail to discern any at this juncture Ms Swoop. I will give it proper consideration in more comfortable surroundings, with tasty victuals and a flask or two of good beech seed wine. In such a fashion I can weigh the pros and cons, thus and so, and exercise the impeccable judgement for which I have made my name on the Raptor Range. This beach is no place for a proper evaluation."

She conjured a scything insult then pursed her beak and stamped a foot instead. "We remain a partnership until this matter is resolved. As you have a flexible attitude toward honour and cannot be trusted not to slink off under cover of darkness, we will find lodgings together."

Chimango wrinkled his beak distastefully. "Be warned Ms Swoop, there is a limit to the opprobrium I will suffer from the beak of a charmless waterfowl. Do not seek that limit out."

❋ ❋ ❋

"I am not comfortable with our room sharing arrangement, Professor Swoop." Chimango sipped a draft of wine from his goblet.

"You have brought the necessity upon yourself and the matter is easily resolved. Hand me the kagu plumage and I will seek lodgings elsewhere."

Chimango chuckled. "If you were one of my pupils I'd award you a distinction for oafish perseverance."

"If you were my lecturer I would lodge myself in another academy," retorted Swoop, draining her own goblet.

A waitress cleared the plates and cutlery from their table. Chimango ordered another flask of wine. Swoop scowled.

"I hope your loutish drinking doesn't extend to snoring. I am a delicate creature. And as there is only one bed in our room, I also trust you will not complain too noisily about the hardness of the floor," she said.

"From the comfort of the sole bed I will have nothing to complain about Professor. And as you will be roosting on the floor tonight, I make it clear now that I do not expect to be issued with reports, complaints or protests. I sleep best against a backdrop of respectful silence."

"There is not the slimmest chance I will be surrendering a night's sleep to your uncouth whims Professor Chimango."

"Nor will I yield my comfort to your churlish demands, Professor Swoop."

"Fine."

"Fine."

❋ ❋ ❋

Chimango lay on his back staring at the ceiling. He was appalled with himself. Perhaps the wine had been at fault for muddling his brain? It was impossible to work out how the unwanted act of sharing his bed with a lanky, cantankerous ibis had turned into a mating.

For reasons he could not even attempt to fathom—drowsy, half in a dream, he'd imagined he was couching with the other Professor Swoop. Alia Swoop the handsome saker falcon, whose beauty, radiant charm and effervescent personality could not stand in higher contrast to the meanness of this witless bird. He'd somehow been transported back a night and deluded himself, substituting the namesake Swoop for the gorgeous falcon Swoop, thus engaging in wild, reckless courtship.

Thankfully the ibis was gone from their chamber on some errand. He would preen, eat and avoid mentioning their shameless tryst, consign it to the worst of memories and move on. It was far too disturbing to linger in reminiscence. As long as he bunked with this appalling creature he promised himself to avoid alcoholic beverages.

She joined him at breakfast and was subdued, avoiding eye contact. They ate a silent meal of seeds and grains with berries, Swoop mostly playing with her food while Chimango consumed his with appetite but not with pleasure.

"I just want to make something perfectly clear," she said, finally. "Last night was an aberration. My wits were befuddled by wine. In the dark I imagined you were someone else. I'm thoroughly ashamed of myself and have zero interest in any sort of repeat performance. Just so that you know."

Chimango nodded. "I was similarly out of sorts. There will be no repeat. I am not remotely attracted to you or your species. Frankly I find you austere and crass, bereft of that provocative warmth that draws male to female and adds dimension to the character."

"You nurture your vanity in a void of wisdom. You would be better rewarded channelling these efforts into self-improvement, Professor Chimango. As an aside your mesonoxian innovations are equally coarse and clumsy."

"Your own amorous deviations lack self-respect. But let us move on. I have now fully considered from multiple angles the question of the kagu plumage. I decree that it will be stuffed and installed at Buzzard Academy in perpetuity as a relic of a lost species, so nearly rescued but for the bumbling efforts of Merlin academics."

Swoop smiled. "I anticipated this outcome and have already secured the plumage for Merlin Museum. A word of advice, Professor— drinking does you no favours, the early bird gets the worm."

Chimango stared bitterly at her. "You rifled my belongings while I slept and stole from me! Have you no shame, Professor Swoop?"

"Behold your own shamelessness before you lecture on the topic. We had an honour agreement that you were happy to violate."

"I demand the return of my property!"

"It was only *your* property in the most abstract sense, Professor Chimango. We had an agreement to share the spoils of our escapade."

"And how does your devious procurement and singular guardianship of the item constitute sharing?"

"I will reflect on the question."

❋ ❋ ❋

"Kagu plumage!" exclaimed Mr Dickenshaw, Tailer. "Well yes, we do carry kagu in store but our stocks are starting to run low."

"There's been a run on kagu plumage," announced Mrs Dickenshaw, matter of factly. "Hard to fathom. Rare bird to best seller. Bingo!"

"Very popular line," agreed Mr Dickenshaw.

"Who's to say what's next with fashion!" Mrs Dickenshaw rolled her eyes, bobbed her crest and tut-tutted.

"You don't by any chance have the yellow spotted version of this plumage?" asked Swoop.

"Oh no. Extinct bird. Long extinct. Well apart from the specimen that escaped from the university. No, we don't carry extinct animals. Completely pointless…"

"No customers," Mrs Dickenshaw finished the sentence.

"I'll take a standard adult, white please," said Swoop.

"For a friend is it? Do you know their size?"

"Whatever you have is fine."

"That's no way to fit plumage," protested Mr Dickenshaw. "I'm a tailer, not some cheap importer of mass produced feathers."

"Quite right," replied Swoop. "My friend is…" she indicated a height similar to her own, "something roughly my size please."

❋ ❋ ❋

Swoop handed Chimango the plumage.

"What's this? he queried, astonished.

"Yellow spotted kagu. I dyed some standard plumage. Stitched on some white feathers. Indistinguishable from the real thing."

"So it's a copy?"

"Yes."

"A cheap rip-off copy?"

"Indistinguishable from the real thing."

"But you're keeping the original and you expect me to present this copy to my academy and pretend it's real plumage?"

"I could have given you nothing at all. In fact I'm starting to wish I had done just that. If the copy is indistinguishable from the actual plumage, what's the problem?"

Chimango nodded. "Good point, Professor Swoop. If you're so happy with the copy, I'll take the original plumage."

"Ha!" said Swoop. "I contacted the Merlin Academy and informed them I have the original plumage. It's impossible to swap them back now."

"Your scheme lacks any vestige of merit, Professor Swoop."

"Then it is an excellent fit to your purpose, Professor Chimango."

7 | Bird in the Hand

"I see little point in our continued room sharing arrangement, Professor Chimango." Swoop took a measured sip of her wine. "We both have a version of the yellow spotted kagu plumage, our account is settled, our partnership void."

"And yet I am not satisfied with my side of the bargain. Nor am I confident that you won't furtively exit before the matter is settled to our mutual satisfaction. *Thurbinger's Law of Equilibrious Harmony* must have the final say."

Chimango eyed her over the top of his goblet as he quaffed its contents. Any quantity of wine failed to improve her cadaverous aspect. He wondered how two birds with the same name and qualifications could be so profoundly dissimilar. One remarkable for her beauty, warmth, intellect and sweet nature, the other for her gauche appearance, effrontery, lumbering manners and ham-fisted cunning. He signalled the waitress to replenish his carafe.

"The point is moot, Professor. Ms

Hoopoe, the Merlin Academy bursar, will be here in a day or two to collect the plumage. You may pursue your metaphysical debate with her."

Chimango wrinkled his nose. "I'm curious to learn what became of your collaborator, Dr Plump, given that her ward, the luckless kagu, perished in such gruesome circumstances?"

"*Dr Plume*... and that is a mystery I'd like an answer to myself. Your colleague Melon also disappeared, no?"

"Professor Talon was being sought by the local magpies. I'm confident he found a way to elude them. He's a master of disguise."

"Plume is also a genius in that regard."

Chimango shrugged nonchalantly. "Or *was* also a genius in that regard. Her own plumage may have washed up on another shoreline."

"We shall see," responded Swoop.

The evening wore on and Swoop eventually retired to their bed chamber leaving Chimango to finish his beech seed wine. Mulling over the events of the day it occurred to him that she may have secreted the kagu plumage somewhere nearby, given that she had no contacts or alternative residences in Rookery.

He sauntered over to the bar and hailed the innkeeper, a portly wood pigeon. "My colleague Professor Swoop, left a bag with you I believe? She needs its contents for a few minutes."

The innkeeper nodded and went out to a back room, returning with a blue satchel. Chimango thanked him and went upstairs to their room. Leaving the satchel just outside the door and hiding the yellow plumage under a wing, he entered. Swoop was facing away, a lump in the bed. He deftly swapped the plumage in his Dickenshaw Tailer bag and placed that in the satchel which he took back to the innkeeper.

Chimango finished his wine in an excellent mood and retired for the night.

❅ ❅ ❅

Unbelievably it had happened again. In the dead of night when starlight and a waxen moon turned birds into silver outlines yet hid their features in shadow, Swoop reminded him again of Swoop. Her smell and her warmth, even her voice, softened in a half sleeping state, was that of his beloved Alia. And she accepted him as Chuck Chimango, the ardent lover, exultant in passion. It was an uncanny transformation.

The harsh morning light however, brought regret. She was the ibis again, her gaunt face and haughty look of disdain, her beady eyes. It was all far too confusing. Chimango sighed and stared at the ceiling.

His mood, though, regained its lift by breakfast.

"I too have summoned an emissary from my academy," he told her between mouthfuls, "Gizzard-Stone, the ornithology dean. He will be here in a day or so to escort the plumage back to Buzzard."

Swoop looked confused. "So you have decided to accept the duplicate plumage?"

Chimango smiled and shrugged happily. "In a manner of speaking... things have a way of working themselves out."

Swoop stared at him through slitted eyes and pursed beak. "What are you up to, Professor Chimango?"

"Up to? What a suspicious ibis we are today my dear! I am merely buoyed by the excellent weather in these parts and the fact that our collaboration will soon, happily, be drawing to a close. My eyrie at the Academy has a commanding view of the Raptor Range. I look forward to standing at that vista again, sooner rather than later."

❊ ❊ ❊

The falcon and the ibis waited on Rookery Wharf and watched passengers disembarking from the Aviary to Rookery service. Swoop stepped forward to greet an officious looking guineafowl with glasses and bright red wattles. Chimango took the bag of a royal flycatcher, his exotic red and blue crest a sharp contrast to his sour expression and surly manner.

Perfunctory introductions were performed, Hoopoe and Gizzard-Stone giving each other narrow looks that hinted at a less than friendly rivalry. The four then made their way to the Grouse Inn for refreshments where they occupied a corner booth in the restaurant.

"Where is Talon in all this," demanded Gizzard-Stone.

"I was rather hoping he'd made his way back to the Academy," said Chimango. "Hasn't been seen since the night the kagu escaped.

There were magpies looking for him."

"So he wasn't involved in the kagu escape?"

"He returned to our lodgings that night so it seems unlikely. The plan was to head with the kagu directly to a designated rendezvous point if the enterprise was successful."

"And you were at this rendezvous?" Gizzard-Stone probed.

"Ah, not quite... had to change the plan on the fly, an unexpected twist in the plot. One must be flexible with this cloak and dagger stuff." Chimango tapped his beak to make the point that he was a seasoned bird of intrigue.

"But Dr Plume succeeded?" Hoopoe addressed Swoop.

"There is no other conclusion. She didn't return to our lodgings and the kagu escaped," responded Swoop.

"And you had no arrangement in your plan to rendezvous with her after the rescue?" continued Hoopoe.

"Well, yes, but, unforeseen circumstances meant I had to withdraw from that part of the mission. My role involved distracting the bird's keepers with a complex and dangerous ruse. I had to improvise and innovate according to the situation," Swoop offered defensively.

"Professor Swoop and I encountered each other by chance the next morning and discovered that we were engaged in similar missions. It was apparent that her mission had been luckier than ours so I convinced her to combine resources for a share of the spoils," Chimango informed his dean.

"Coerced," interrupted Swoop. "Professor Chimango threatened to reveal our involvement in the kagu's escape to the local magpies. I had no choice but to agree," she explained to Hoopoe.

Chimango chuckled and nodded at Gizzard-Stone. "Professor Swoop was initially aloof to the prospect of collaboration and needed convincing. One uses whatever leverage one has in such delicate negotiations."

"We went in search of Dr Plume and her ward but found only the kagu's plumage and some odd marks on the beach. The kagu came to a grisly end. There was no sign of Dr Plume," Swoop elaborated.

"And you think it's unlikely this Merlin doctor and the kagu escaped alive, Chimango?" asked Gizzard-Stone with a note of skepticism.

"The bird was delaminated, Dean. One struggles to visualise a circumstance where that has played out well."

"So you have the plumage?" Hoopoe asked Swoop.

"Yes," replied Swoop.

"Hold on a moment. Chimango—you said you have the plumage?" inter-rupted Gizzard-Stone with a look of consternation.

"I do," responded Chimango, suavely.

"He has a tailered copy of the plumage," said Swoop. "I have the original plumage, naturally."

"Do you?" chuckled Chimango. "Sometimes the juiciest worms are found by the late bird."

Swoop raised her eyebrows in alarm. She leapt to her feet and rushed to the bar, signalling the innkeeper. A few moments later she returned with her blue satchel looking visibly relieved.

"The plumage is intact. Professor Chimango has a morbid sense of humour," she announced, perching back on her seat.

Chimango winked at Gizzard-Stone with a broad grin.

"Who has the authentic plumage and who has the copy?" Gizzard-Stone grumbled at Chimango.

"Let us retire to a private room and find out," said Chimango.

The four made their way to the chamber where Chimango extracted his plumage from the tailer bag and laid it out on the bed. Swoop pulled hers from the satchel and spread it out beside Chimango's. They were, to all intents and purposes, identical.

"I see no difference," complained Gizzard-Stone.

"And yet mine is the original. Hers is, admittedly, a rather good copy, but a fake nonetheless. Deep feather analysis will confirm that to be the case."

"Professor Chimango has a reputation for cloddish deceptions, Bursar," said Swoop to Hoopoe, pursing her beak. "I can guarantee mine is the garment worn by the deceased kagu. Its authenticity is beyond any question or doubt."

"Or *was* before the innkeeper handed me your satchel for safe keeping Professor Swoop. Now mine is the more likely candidate," laughed Chimango.

"Liar," retorted Swoop.

"Still, I am happy with the present distribution of plumage. I do not wish to swap," responded Chimango. "Shall we take our leave

Dean?" he said, turning to Gizzard-Stone.

"There must be a quick way of determining which set of plumage is authentic and which is fake," said Gizzard-Stone.

"There is an obvious way to do that," said Swoop. "Since embarking on this adventure I have become somewhat expert in Rhynochetidae morphology and cladistic analysis. If someone would care to birdwalk these garments I can determine in an instant which is which."

"I too have no small expertise in this obscure branch of ornithology," added Chimango breezily. "And I do not trust either of the Merlin employees to handle our plumage. Professor Swoop is a known con artist and Ms Hoopoe has a shifty look."

"I urge you to remain vigilant—do not let our plumage out of your sight for a second Ms Hoopoe," Swoop cautioned. "Professor Chimango and his flamboyant sidekick are doubtless planning another subterfuge. One learns to tread warily around saker falcons and their allies."

Gizzard-Stone scowled. "So be it," he exclaimed.

He snatched Chimango's plumage and went behind the dressing screen. Hoopoe took Swoop's into the bathroom.

A short time later two yellow spotted kagus emerged from their dressing enclosures. Chimango's eyes went wide and his jaw dropped.

"Where are the dean and the bursar?" he demanded, agog. "Who are you two? How did two yellow spotted kagus find their way here?"

Swoop blinked rapidly. "This is impossible!"

Gizzard-Stone shook his head in annoyance. "Have you two lost your wits? I am Professor Gizzard-Stone and we're trying to determine which of us has authentic plumage."

Chimango stared at Gizzard-Stone, then at Hoopoe, then at Swoop.

"Two kagus?" she silently mouthed at him.

The door burst open and a tide of magpies swept into the room.

"Nobody move," barked one.

"You're all under arrest," shouted another.

"Cuff them," ordered a third.

SPRING EDITION

the journal of birdology

NOT EXTINCT!

The Lost World — a population of 'extinct' bird species found alive and well
Plume & Talon

PLUS

Dismal Owlbane
Parasite of the Sandy Scops Owl
Tuwoo, et al.

Breeding Programme
Yellow Spotted Kagu Recovery
Interview with Xerxes Tweet

8 | Breeding Programme

The ***Journal of Birdology*** interviewed Senior Professor Xerxes Tweet about the University of Rookery's Yellow Spotted (Tweet's) Kagu Conservation Programme. In *JoB's* Winter Edition we documented a single specimen of this archaic species under the protection of UoR and a joint breeding initiative with the Merlin Academy. Two animals are now under Professor Tweet's care at Rookery and an in-house breeding programme is in full swing.

JoB: Your first kagu escaped Professor?

Tweet: Our original specimen was not a happy bird. Clinically insane. Self-harming. Not wonderful breeding material—but you take what you can get with a species previously listed as extinct. There was some sort of "rescue" attempt, a fanatical bird liberation group I presume. We were holding the bird against his will, yes, but trying to save his species. He disappeared without a trace. There are rumours he stole a boat and perished on the reef but we have no way to confirm or disprove that.

JoB: So how did Rookery acquire two replacement kagus?

Tweet: An excellent question indeed. The details are somewhat vague. Our working hypothesis is that two more kagus from their tiny breeding group came in search of their missing comrade. They were too late, of course, our bird had flown. But even with this expansion of the known population from one to three, we have to assume the species still teeters on extinction. We were able to capture them and put them under around-the-clock supervised protection at our facility.

JoB: You have a male and a female?

Tweet: Yes, breeding age, both fertile and in good health. Amazing luck really. They share our kagu enclosure, which is a very intimate space.

JoB: And have they shown any interest in mating?

Tweet: Not yet. They don't really seem to get along. The male is surly and truculent, the female caustic and critical. Indeed, their arguments and tantrums have become background noise in that enclosure, it's really something to behold. But we're still hopeful. Two or three years of close proximity. It's hard to imagine they won't breed.

JoB: You mentioned your last bird was clinically insane. What is the mental condition of this pair?

Tweet: Delusion seems to be a bit of a theme with Tweet's kagus. My theory is that the pressure of being perpetually endangered in a small gene pool has led to mental fragility in the species. The pair emphatically deny they're kagus and have even made up wild stories about being employees of far flung academies. It would make excellent comedy if it wasn't ultimately so tragic.

JoB: And if they do breed, what then?

Tweet: Kagu are a long lived species with a sustained fertility arc. They mate for life. The female is younger than the male so the prospect of annual broods is excellent. This pair could regenerate their species. It's an exciting project.

❋ ❋ ❋

Professor Alia Swoop tossed the letter into her waste paper basket. Another inquiry from the insufferable Professor Chimango regarding a non-existent Merlin professor, Alia Swoop, *saker falcon*.

It was obvious the "Swoop" who toyed with him in his squalid tryst had then fobbed the old satyr off with a false identity. And annoyingly ironic that it was her name and title sequestered for the duplicity, particularly given their later unhappy dealings with one another. Life, she mused, has a way of confronting you with certain mistakes you'd rather forget.

Compounding things further, her own efforts to locate the utterly charming Prof. Chuck Chimango, *ibis*, had fallen flat. She nursed a niggling suspicion that *saker falcon* Chimango was intercepting and destroying her missives out of some sense of vendetta or sheer perversity. It was vexing—to say the very least—that her dashing paramour shared a name and address with that detestable bird.

Associate Professor Gentoo backed into the office, her wings full of administrative documents. She swivelled and dumped a good portion of them into Swoop's intray.

"I never imagined I'd miss our bursar," quipped Swoop. "Are we all getting a bundle of her work or am I being singled out as some form of ongoing punishment for losing her in Rookery?"

"Ms Hoopoe was smug, ambitious and overbearing, but she was an efficient guineafowl with the accounts," replied Gentoo. "Is there any news of her whereabouts or did she find the speckled hen of her dreams in Birdland and elope with the academy funds?"

"Her disappearance was as abrupt as it was unconventional. She went into the bathroom, a kagu emerged from the bathroom. I was then annoyingly taken into custody by some officious magpies and when I returned the next day there was no sign of her anywhere. Not even a note."

"Strange indeed." Gentoo shuffled from one foot to the other as penguins do. "There's another article about the Great Non-Extinction by Professor Plume—in the Spring Edition of *Journal of Birdology*. Have you seen it?"

"Yes, remarkable stuff! I wonder how she located her island of extinct birds in the first place? Last seen escaping Birdland with a kagu under her wing. Moments later, leading the greatest ornithological revolution of all time!"

Gentoo nodded. "I wonder how she got stuck with that gyrfalcon on her adventure. I'd be surprised if he contributes anything more than his name to their research!"

"Engaging in your life's great work in league with a pompous raptor must be extremely vexing for her. I know it would drive me insane," Swoop agreed with a sneer.

❄ ❄ ❄

Chimango stood at the window surveying the view from his new eyrie at the top of the Buzzard Academy's southeast cupola. His recent promotion to ornithology dean had meant a relocation to the spacious suite vacated by Gizzard-Stone.

Professor Rouke perched at Chimango's desk reading the *Journal of Birdology*. He paused midway through the leading article.

"So Emeritus Professor Talon has still to reveal the whereabouts of his mysterious lost world?"

"He's keeping the location close to his chest," affirmed Chimango. "And why wouldn't he? He's sitting on the most momentous discovery in modern ornithology. There's even talk of a big budgie movie, *Moas in the Mist* with Falco Alopex and Desdemona Fez touted for the leading roles."

"It does make fascinating reading. More a detective novel than a set of scholarly research papers."

"Meanwhile, the Buzzard Academy is doing very well from his updates in the journals. Enrolments here are at an all time high," mused Chimango. "Rookery's breeding pair of archaic kagus barely makes the news with all the buzz Talon and his coauthor are generating."

"It's truly remarkable how yesterday's hottest news story is today's wrapping paper," Rouke chuckled. "I take it we're no closer to solving Gizzard-Stone's mysterious disappearance?"

"Complete enigma. I was in the room with him, he went behind a screen and *poof*, vanished. Uncanny. Then two yellow spotted kagus walked in, followed by every magpie in Rookery. Absolute circus. That awful Swoop creature from the Merlin and I were arrested too. They had to let us go, of course, we were clearly just bystanders to the fiasco. And in fairness to the magpies, everything about that horrid ibis screeches duplicity... beady shifty eyes, slippery manner, rustic appearance. I would have arrested her too in their place."

Rouke nodded. "There are one or two academics at this facility who'll be quietly happy if Gizzard-Stone stays disappeared. Our erstwhile dean was not the most popular bird to hold the post... not naming any names, of course, but Professor Tuwoo's demeanour is decidedly less defensive since his departure and Dr Prettyboy has shed his querulous melancholy."

"I hope to garner more collegial respect in the role of dean than my predecessor. Gizzard-Stone set a low benchmark in that regard."

"You have my full support, Professor."

Chimango smiled and nodded. "We still have to fill our lecturer vacancies—this becomes an urgent matter with an approaching semester. I've tried in vain to locate a certain professor of ornithology at the Merlin—a very talented saker falcon—to see if I can tempt her into accepting a post here. But alas, I am constantly referred to her ibis namesake, which is the equivalent of standing hoodless in a monsoon of warm droppings. You should hope for your own sake that you never brush against that rancorous bird on a midnight stroll.

"I, thankfully, was caressed by the fates—that gangly banshee was slinking about the Rookery night too! On another night we might even have crossed paths!" Chimango shuddered. "But my starlit encounter was seraphic, an appointment with a celestial wonder. Ah, how bitter that our union was so ephemeral. She, an apparition, a dream, a fascination, now just an exquisite memory, the fading embers of..."

"Are there many applicants, Dean?" Rouke cut across Chimango's all too familiar reminiscence to change the subject.

"The usual suspects," Chimango sighed. "That bird who applies for every vacant position we notify, the ornithomusicologist."

"Fluttertongue. Hmmm. I read her aimless dissertation on twin-syrinx interference patterns collapsing the chirp function. It gave me a headache."

"Quite. And there's a résumé from a Birdland junior, Associate Professor Keel. His thesis is titled *Ratite Locomotion in Urban Settings*. He states on his job application—rather brazenly—that he believes he's being stifled by the "old guard of professors" in his academic post at Rookery. The reference I obtained from Brightfeather, describes him as 'a precocious upstart'."

"Not promising," grimaced Rouke. "Doesn't sound much like a team player."

"There's one from a Merlin ibis whose graduate thesis was *Statistical analysis of Louse Distribution Curves in Medium-Sized Puffin Colonies*. She has a glowing reference from a certain notorious professor at that academy. Her application was filed unceremoniously in the waste paper bin without reading." Chimango shook his head to dislodge an imaginary bad taste.

"We do have one very promising candidate though, a paleornithologist, one Miss Luciwa Peregrine. A rather striking banded kestrel." He winked at his collegue conspiratorially. "She comes with the highest recommendations too, from Professor Talon, no less. Let's hope we can secure her services."

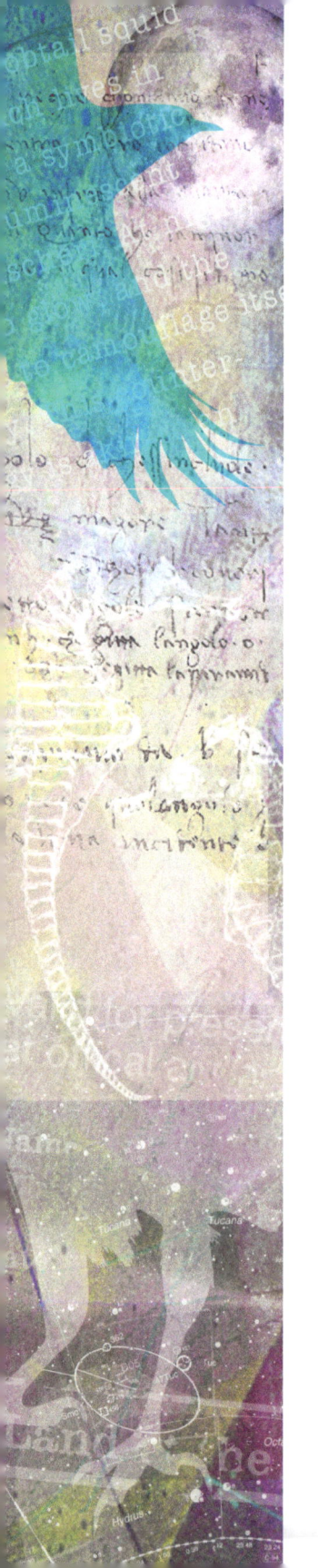

Epilogue | Flotsam

She could feel pressure on her back and the tingle of a watery sun on her face. An orange blackness inside her eyelids was the sort where descending luminescent dots jump back to the top when they reach the bottom of your eyes.

She could hear the sea—small waves lapping on the side of the boat. There was an aroma too, tropical scents mingling with seaweed and brine.

The lump of somnolent warmth named George Ballchaser III was pressing against her calf, twitching through his dreams as the small boat rocked gently, cradling them both.

Lucy opened her eyes, yawned and stretched. She looked around. They were bobbing in the middle of a small bay surrounded by coconut trees and a curving sandy beach. An anchored raft was only a few feet away from the *Luciana*. It was constructed out of barrels lashed together with vines and weathered planks, a small hut in the centre.

It was the next morning of their adventure and that meant her birthday must be tomorrow. She decided not to wake George Ballchaser III to tell him the incredible news. Hopefully he'd remember anyway and bark "hap-py-birth-day-to-mor-row, to-you" or something equally appropriate.

Lucy leaned over the side of the boat and peered into the water. It was crystal clear and near the sea floor among rocks, anemones, bryozoans and waving kelp she saw a pair of gannets wearing glass helmets pretending to be fish. A kingfisher in a rakish helmet came into view, then she saw some seagulls turtling across the scene and a school of sparrows darting in pointless zigzags.

She giggled. "I hope you can swim under the water as well as you can on top of it George Ballchaser the Third."

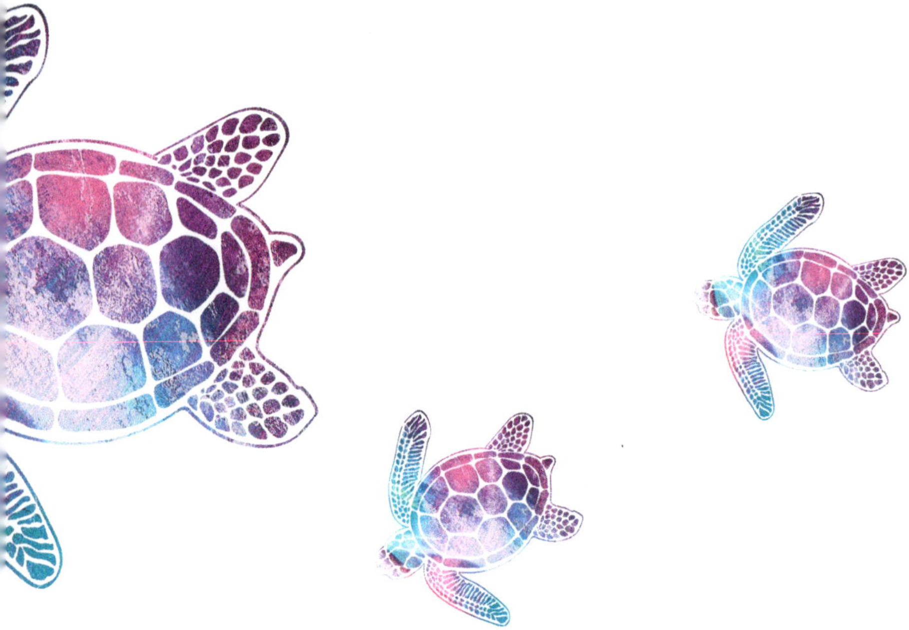

nuna
www.nunagallery.com

NUNA

CPSIA information can be obtained
at www.ICGtesting.com
Printed in the USA
LVHW071658210821
695828LV00012B/374/J